Leviathan

L.S. JOHNSON

Traversing Z Press
San Leandro, California
www.traversingz.com

ISBN: 978-0-9988936-2-4
Library of Congress Control Number: 2018905541

TABLE OF CONTENTS

Canst thou draw out leviathan with an hook?
or his tongue with a cord which thou lettest down?
Canst thou put an hook into his nose?
or bore his jaw through with a thorn?
Will he make many supplications unto thee?
will he speak soft words unto thee?
Will he make a covenant with thee?
wilt thou take him for a servant for ever?
—Job 41:1–4

PART I

Home

CHAPTER I

The Woman on the Road

I first saw merely a flutter of movement far down the road. Perhaps an animal, for what else would be there? The road led nowhere save the ruins of Harkworth Hall, and that had burned months ago. Anything worth salvaging had been salvaged. The property was now mired in legal battles, perhaps never to be inhabited again. Even the road was fading away to rutted tracks in the dirt.

I renewed my focus on the task at hand—but then the fluttering became a cloak and the cloak stumbled with a cry that reached even my distant ears, at which point Mr. Windham used my distraction to deliver a punch to my shoulder.

"I have warned you, Miss Daniels," he said. "Your wandering attention will be your undoing, far more than your size or lack of skill. Any opponent will use it against you, and not just to knock you off your feet."

Ruefully, I took a moment to catch my breath. We made an odd pair: a greying, scarred man stripped to his shirtsleeves, head bare despite the chill, sparring with a woman three decades his junior in a woolen dress and petticoats. Eight days of lessons in defense and I was beginning to wonder if I would ever again be without bruises. Still, I glanced at the road once more. Now there was no movement. Had I imagined it?

"I thought I saw something," I said, but the words sounded poor even to my ears.

"Oh? Is Miss Chase distracting you again?"

At the amusement in his voice I blushed. For our first appointment, Jo had set herself to watching us until at last I begged her not to. Having her witness every misstep, every poor block and hesitant lunge, made it impossible to give my full attention to Mr. Windham's lessons—lessons, he told me sternly, designed to preserve my life, not to impress observers. Once she absented herself, my skills began improving, but I had not been able to undo Mr. Windham's initial impression.

Though, in truth, there was nothing to insinuate. Since she had taken up residence in our house just three weeks ago, Jo had been the perfect guest: polite, helpful, attentive to my father … and in no way overly attentive to me. To look at her now was to see a demure Englishwoman, not the bold spy who had masked her sex to catch a murderer. One would take her for a mere acquaintance, save for the occasional searching look she gave me, or the heat that seemed to arise from our most casual touch. Just our hands brushing made us jump like startled cats—

But I was becoming distracted again.

We resumed our stances, kicking a few stray rocks out of our patch of flattened grass. The wind was cold, but I was forbidden a cloak; bad enough, Mr. Windham declared, that I insisted on wearing skirts. "These men won't fence with you, Miss Daniels," he had said with exasperation. "They fight to kill, and they will use every advantage, including your clothing." Yet what else could I do? Jo and I were tasked with infiltrating Thomas Masterson's shipping company, and our plan was to pretend to be man and wife. Jo would join his company as a clerk and I would maintain our respectability while aiding her investigation. I had no reason to wear breeches, and in truth, I did not want to.

Though Mr. Windham had a point. While he moved with practiced ease, the stances he first taught me had set my skirts tangling around my legs. Wearing any kind of hoop was a further hindrance. After some experimentation, we devised different movements to keep my skirts from twisting, though there was still the worry an opponent might use the loose fabric against me. But at least I would surprise assailants expecting meekness, and we hoped that in a few more weeks I might learn to capitalize on that astonishment.

"Begin," Mr. Windham barked, and I raised my fists—

—when suddenly the cloak appeared again, closer this time and making unerringly for our house.

"There is someone!" I hurried past Mr. Windham, who punched the air with a muttered curse. For a moment I thought it might be Jo, only she had said she was going to the village, to post some letters and start planning our removal to Medby. What would she be doing at the Hall?

When at last I could make out the woman's face, however, I recognized her at once. She was the wife of one of the fishermen who lived on the far side of the village. Her face was pale and damp, her skirts clutched in her hands.

As she drew close she slowed. "Miss Daniels," she gasped, "if you could—some water—"

"Of course!" I caught her arm to steady her, for she was trembling violently. "It is Missus Owston, is it not?"

"Yes, miss," she said, forcing the words out. "What day is it?"

I stared at her, astonished. "Why, it's Wednesday, Missus Owston."

At that, her face drained of color and Mr. Windham rushed to her other side to help keep her upright.

"Oh God! I've been gone since yesterday," she whispered, tears spilling over her cheeks. "How will I ever explain? Oh God, save me! Harry is going to kill me."

We had her settled in the kitchen with Mrs. Simmons pouring her a brandy when a clatter told me Jo had returned. She was forever catching her skirts on the edges of doors and furniture, seemingly unable to traverse a room without shifting objects in her path. Her cheeks were flushed and her grey eyes were alight. "Caroline!" she cried upon seeing me. "Caroline, we may have to go sooner—"

She broke off, however, when I indicated Mrs. Owston's hunched form. "What happened?" she asked.

"She arrived at the house nearly in a faint," I said. "From the Hall road," I added significantly.

At my words, Jo's face became serious. She put down her basket and carefully laid her bonnet over it, hiding the papers inside. "What were you doing there?" she asked.

Mrs. Owston began weeping again. “I didn’t want to go,” she said. “But a pound! Just to show him the way!”

I started to speak but Jo gave a little shake of her head. “Who?” she asked, her tone gentle.

“I don’t know. A foreign gentleman.” She took a shuddering breath. “Someone at the pub had given him Harry’s name, but Harry’s boat had sailed. So, I brought him to the road, but then he said I was to take him to the Hall itself. But when we got there, he wanted to see the bay where it got stove in, and when I tried to leave, he said he would not pay me unless I went with him to the bay.”

She wept harder then. Jo started to speak, but this time I shook my head. Instead she sat, fidgeting, while I helped Mrs. Owston take another sip of brandy and coaxed her into eating a biscuit. The food and drink seemed to revive her.

“I took him all the way to the bay, though now it was getting on and I was tired from all the walking. I took him right where it all collapsed. But when I asked for my money, it was as if he couldn’t hear me. He just kept staring at the water. I told him if he didn’t pay I would go back and fetch my husband, and he looked at me—!” She clenched her eyes shut for a moment. “Oh, I thought he was going to throw me in! And then he said, ‘so it’s true,’ and he asked me if I knew any women who had died there. Oh, my blood ran cold! I was so frightened! I just started running, and I suppose—I suppose I fell, because next I knew it was morning. Only, my arm hurt terribly, and I realized I was holding something.”

She drew a pound coin from her pocket. The surface was stained brown, and she pushed up her sleeve to show a large cut running across her forearm. Mrs. Simmons made a dismayed sound and set about washing the ugly wound. I shuddered at the sight, instinctively rubbing the scar on my palm, a testament to my similar encounter last spring. Then, my blood-soaked handkerchief had attracted a monster. Had Mrs. Owston's gentleman tried to do the same?

"Oh, he was a madman, a madman!" Mrs. Owston wept. "Only what will Harry think, with me staying out all night?"

"He won't think anything, because we will explain," I began, only to be interrupted by a cough from Mrs. Simmons. She waved me towards the hall, leaving Jo to fuss over Mrs. Owston.

"I wouldn't get involved, Miss," she said in a low voice.

"What do you mean?"

"To put it plainly? Harold Owston is a drunk, and a mean one. He thinks what he likes, and anyone trying to change his mind will only get fisticuffs for their trouble." She nodded at the kitchen. "The best thing for her is to simply bear it and hope it passes quickly."

"But surely, if we all go—Jo, Mister Windham …" I trailed off, for her expression hardened when I spoke Jo's name.

"Well," she said. "You'll do as you please, I'm sure."

She turned on her heel and strode back into the kitchen, leaving me bewildered and saddened. Over the past week, Mrs. Simmons had been visibly irritated any time I objected to her suggestions, especially when my alternative involved Jo. Was she angry at myself, or Jo? They had not quarreled to my knowledge, and yet … but my musings were interrupted when Mr. Windham touched my arm, once more bewigged and in his coat.

"Miss Chase met the post in the village. She has brought me a letter, which I suspect echoes the dispatch for you." His voice was somber. "I must leave. Tensions are rising between France and England, and another of Masterson's ships was lost. This time, some of the crew were saved. They claim it was seized by the French, though the French deny this."

"But that cannot be," I exclaimed. "Why would the French resort to such tactics? They have no need of it, and it would only push matters to a breaking point."

"Indeed. Either the French are preparing to move against us, or Thomas Masterson wants people to believe they are—and he's making a good job of it." He smiled ruefully. "It seems today was our last lesson, Miss Daniels. Mister Smith has asked the Navy to station ships in Grimsby, just below Medby, in case Masterson acts. I am to meet the commander there, to inform him that he may be facing a monster equal parts serpent and squid and capable of destroying his fleet. You and Miss Chase are to make your way to Medby as soon as possible."

"Oh." I realized I was wringing my hands and buried them in my skirts. "I—I see." But that was not what I wanted to say; what I wanted to say was, *it's much too soon, I'm not ready!*

Yet I had not been ready for Edward Masterson, either, and I was still alive—alive, and with Jo at my side. Surely his brother could be no worse.

CHAPTER II

Foreigners

Mrs. Owston refused all offers of help save for us taking her home. While Mr. Simmons hitched up the carriage, Mrs. Simmons properly bandaged her arm, and I added some shillings to the pound and put it all in a little purse. As I helped her to the cart, I looked back at the house to see Mrs. Simmons speaking sharply to Jo, Jo's face darkly furious.

"You stay out of it," Mrs. Simmons was saying as I hurried back to them. "You'll only make things worse for her."

"I only mean to ascertain if her foreigner was a Frenchman," Jo said, but her expression belied her light tone.

"Besides, if we verify her story, surely Mister Owston will have no cause for anger," I put in.

"I am telling you, Miss: you will only make it worse." Mrs. Simmons looked from myself to Jo. "Emily was popular among the lads down at the inn, Harry Owston among them, and they never were told the truth of how she died; they only know she met Edward Masterson in this house. If you want to do Moira Owston a kindness, you and Miss Chase especially mustn't stir him up further." She smoothed down her apron. "Now, I am going to set the table for dinner and wake your father in the study—?"

I felt a rising unease, but I could not speak to Jo because Mr. Windham appeared, leading his horse. "I thought I would ride with you," he said. "We could inquire at the inn about this foreigner."

"My plan exactly," Jo said blithely. "I just need to fetch something."

"What are you going to do?" I demanded.

"Just what I said," she replied, but her eyes would not meet mine. She hurried inside and up the stairs to the guest bedroom she had taken over. She started to shut the door but I was on her heels, and she instead began rifling through the chest she had brought.

"What if Missus Simmons is right?" I asked. "What if our barging in makes things worse?"

She gave me an outraged look. "I never *barge in*! What kind of creature do you take me for?"

"You barge in on me every morning!" I retorted. For it was true: Joanna Chase was an unrepentant early riser, often beating the Simmonses to the kitchen to light the fire, at which point she would fling open my door, deposit her restless, energetic self upon my bed, and start to detail our day.

"And you have barged in on me now," Jo said. She had pulled out half her clothes with such vigor that her hair was coming undone. "It is a testament to our ease with one another. With Moira Owston, I will be a model of decorum—as long as I am met with the same."

Her tone was light, but I glimpsed a small, metallic object which she quickly tucked into her pocket.

"Was that a knife?" I said in what I hoped was a severe tone.

She stood and folded her arms. “It’s only for protection,” she said. “What if our Frenchman is still in the village?”

“Mister Windham says that anyone bringing a weapon to a confrontation expects to use it.”

“Bother Mister Windham.” She tried to push past me.

“He said the latest dispatch advised us to start packing.”

“It *advised* many things.” Her voice still had an edge to it. “But I think our course of action depends on the nationality of the man.”

“Why would anyone come to see a ruin, though?”

“Remember what Missus Owston told us. He said, ‘so it’s true.’ And how he cut her?” She took a step closer to me. “He knows about the beast, Caroline. Perhaps not all of it, perhaps he didn’t quite believe it. But he knew enough to visit the damage it caused and to try that handkerchief trick of Masterson’s.”

“He wants to control it?” I asked.

“Or he’s been threatened by it? A beast that could lay waste to an entire fleet? It would assure victory for the side that could wield it—or afford to pay its master.”

Lost in contemplating these horrible scenarios, I had not realize how her body was brushing mine; but suddenly I was aware, and aware, too, that her cheeks had tinged pink.

“You may have to become Missus Read sooner than anticipated,” she whispered.

“I thought we would have more time to practice,” I replied, and was pleased to see her blush deepen even as my own face reddened. If I had to squirm before her, I could at least make her equally uncomfortable.

I expected some kind of witty retort but instead she took my hand. "How soon can your father be ready?" she asked.

"I suppose soon? A few days? It's not as if we are leaving forever, just for a time." I hesitated when her eyes stayed fixed on my hand. "Yes?"

"If it was indeed a Frenchman, then I think we should leave as soon as possible." Abruptly she dropped my hand and slipped past me into the hall. "I won't be gone long," she said over her shoulder.

"Indeed we won't," I said, following her. When she gave me a horrified look I merely shrugged. "If you get arrested, it will complicate our journey tremendously."

"Caroline," she said in a low voice.

"You can 'Caroline' me all you want," I snapped, finally losing my patience. "But we have an assignment for which I have already accepted a substantial payment, and that may have ramifications for all of England. I have a duty to make sure you act accordingly."

She seemed about to speak, then shrugged and continued down the stairs, her skirts catching on the risers. At the door, she seized a cloak and tossed another at me. "As you wish," she said with a too-broad smile. By the time I tied my cloak on, she was seated in the carriage, chatting to Mr. Windham and Mrs. Owston as if everything was fine.

But nothing was fine, nor would it be.

On our way to the village I let Jo entertain Mrs. Owston. I was totting up all we needed to do to effect our relocation, and the many tasks needed to close up the house—and what of our lodgings in Medby? Could they be ready in advance? What about Jo's position in Thomas Masterson's company? Would it seem strange to appear so soon after our initial letters?

My mind was whirling by the time we reached the village, but when we came in sight of the inn a plan that would prevent any confrontation suddenly presented itself. I asked Mr. Simmons to halt and I disembarked, gesturing for Jo to join me. "Mister Simmons will drive Missus Owston home," I said firmly. "We shall make our inquiries and he can stop for us on his return."

Jo glared at me. "I don't think—"

"Oh, it's quite all right, Miss," Mrs. Owston put in. "You've both done so much for me already. I wouldn't want to put you to further trouble."

"It's no trouble," Jo snapped.

"But we have much to do," I said with an apologetic smile. "Or do I misunderstand our situation?"

She scowled at me, then stormed out of the carriage, pausing to whisper something in Mrs. Owston's ear. I pretended not to see this, and with a last goodbye, I sent the poor woman on her way, only to face a visibly fuming Jo.

"Mister Simmons was a soldier for years," I said before she could speak. "We have work to do."

Without waiting for her reply, I went inside, where Mr. Windham was already conversing with Mr. Pawson, the innkeeper. He was a familiar face from church, and more than happy to help us, if for nothing else than to vent his ire at his former guest.

"He called himself Mister Hunt," he said, showing us the florid signature. "But he was no Englishman. I can spot the French a mile off. Too good for our food, and Missus said he didn't even turn down the blanket! I'll have you know we keep a clean house here."

"You certainly do," Mr. Windham said, "and the lack of food was his loss, I can assure you." As he continued to mollify Mr. Pawson, I looked at Jo, relieved to find some of the anger leeched from her face.

She caught my eye and nodded. "Did he say where he was bound for?"

"Only wanted to know the quickest way south," Mr. Pawson said. "And good riddance."

Medby lay due south. "So, he left yesterday?" I prodded.

The simple question provoked a most voluble response, as Mr. Pawson went into a tirade about the Frenchman's pestering questions regarding last summer, and meanwhile his horses standing ready—

"Last summer?" Jo and I asked in unison.

"Oh, yes," Mr. Pawson said. "Not surprising, considering how often he took a drink." He pointed to his dining room, where even now I could hear the sounds of tankards and glasses. "That's all they talk about in there, you know. Get them in their cups and they'll say anything. Do you know—" He leaned over the counter, shaking his head. "Do you know, some of those lot believe a *snake* came out of the water and ate poor Emily? A snake bigger than a house. Mind you, they also swear they've seen the Princess of Wales dancing with fairies by the coach road." He tapped his forehead.

Mr. Windham drew us aside, keeping his voice low. "I think we must accept Mister Pawson's assessment. It's too risky not to."

"Agreed," Jo said.

"Good. Then I will tell Mister Smith you are on your way and give him the details of what occurred." He led us back outside. "Hopefully Mister Simmons will not be delayed."

We followed his gaze down the road, shielding our eyes from the midday sun; thus, we did not notice the man who had followed us outside until he spoke.

"*You*," the man said. "Where's my wife?"

"Pardon?" I exclaimed as Mr. Windham stepped between us.

"My wife." The man's expression was ugly. "Seen walking to *you*."

"Mister Owston, I believe," Mr. Windham said, raising his hands. "We have seen your wife home. She had a terrible fall and cut herself badly."

The man shook his head; a slow, belligerent movement. "Not you," he grunted. He held up a finger that wavered between Jo and I. "*You*."

"Perhaps you mean me," Jo purred.

"No, he means me," I said quickly. "You must know my father, sir. Theophilus Daniels. He was a regular here."

"Oh, he is talking to me, I am certain of it," Jo said in the same purring voice.

I looked at her. "Don't," I whispered. A crowd was forming on the green, watching us—and did we not have a sworn duty? Were we not agreed on it?

"I think he is talking to me," Mr. Windham put in, "and reminding me that it is my turn to stand a round."

He laid a hand on Mr. Owston's arm, but Mr. Owston shoved him away. In turn, Jo struck Mr. Owston in the chest, sending him stumbling backwards.

"I think he's had enough, Mister Windham," she said. "What he needs isn't in a bottle."

Mr. Owston grabbed her arm and swung her around, making to hit her. Mr. Windham seized him in turn, creating an awkward, straining chain of bodies. I looked around for help, but the villagers simply watched, some visibly amused, some with darker expressions. *They only know she met Edward Masterson in this house.* Did they think us complicit in poor Emily's demise? Or was it just that we were gentlewomen fighting like fishwives?

"We have business," Mr. Owston slurred. "We have business, *bitch*."

"Now that's enough," Mr. Windham said loudly, pulling him backwards. "You have crossed a line, sir; you don't need a drink, you need a dunking."

In response, Mr. Owston kneed him in the groin, then turned and punched Jo, his meaty fist obliterating her face.

The sight of that blow, how she fell to her knees from it, provoked a terrified rage that I had never felt before, not even last spring. I did not think; I simply threw myself bodily against Mr. Owston. My saving grace was that, despite my overwhelming fury, I turned as Mr. Windham had taught me, so I struck Mr. Owston with my shoulder and all my weight behind it. He seemed to fall up, then down, landing with an enormous thud. Still I could not think, and made to throw myself atop him when Mr. Windham's arm caught me about my waist.

"Breathe," he said in my ear. "In—" He waited for my inhalation. "—and out. Again."

I breathed, feeling my nostrils flare with each huge breath, my heart pounding in my chest. Mr. Owston staggered to his feet and I wiggled in Mr. Windham's grasp. If he hit Jo again—

"All right, all right, that's enough." Mr. Pawson came out, wiping his hands on his apron. He looked us over, his frown deepening as he took in Jo's bloody nose, and then he nodded at me. "Go home, Miss Daniels." When Mr. Owston made to lunge forward he placed a hand on his chest. "Take it easy, Harry, or I'll send for the constable. Come back inside."

Jo staggered to her feet, her nose swelling and purpling. "I think the constable—"

"Is not needed," Mr. Windham interrupted. He finally let go of me and I hurried to Jo's side, but when I tried to examine her face she pushed my hands away.

"It's coming," Harry Owston bellowed, his voice suddenly clear. "It came for Emily and it will come again. We have turned away from God." He jabbed a meaty finger at Jo. "We have turned *away.*"

A murmur ran through the crowd—for it was a proper crowd now. Half the village seemed to have gathered. I carefully took Jo's arm. "Come, *cousin,*" I said. "We should be getting home—and you will have some explaining to do on Sunday."

There were few smiles at my weak riposte but something

eased, like an animal retreating. I took the opportunity to draw Jo back a few steps, increasing the distance between her and Mr. Owston.

"Though Sunday is a ways off," Mr. Windham said, "and I, for one, could use a drink. Who's with me?"

There was another murmur, far more cheerful. A few men came up to Mr. Owston and spoke to him, cajoling and scolding him by turns until he turned back to the inn. Mr. Windham fell in behind them, pausing to whisper in my ear, "Go home. I will write."

I steered Jo away, though she kept looking darkly over her shoulder. We waited beneath a bare oak until Mr. Simmons returned. At his startled expression I shook my head and pushed Jo inside, seating myself next to her. She touched her swelling nose gingerly, but it wasn't until we were past the village that she muttered, "What was that, then?"

I glanced at her, but said nothing.

"Cousins, is that what we are?" Her voice was nasally from the swelling.

"It makes things easier," I said.

She leaned back, scowling. "They don't need fictions, they need to deal with their own," she said. "Tell me, then. How are the Harry Owstons and the Mastersons of the world so different from each other? What price our victories, if they come at the expense of women like Moira Owston?"

I hesitated as the import of her words struck me. "They are different in their numbers," I finally said. "Harold Owston harms few. Thomas Masterson may have already murdered dozens, even hundreds."

And it was true, but God help me, it sickened me to say it. I kept thinking of Moira Owston's fear; I thought of poor Emily again, and how my horror at her fate had been mingled with relief that it was not I …

Jo was silent, pushing at her nose, but at last she sighed deeply. "I'm sorry," she said. "That was poor of me. There are no good answers to that question … and you were right, I nearly went for the knife, and where would that have left us?"

I could not answer save to take her hand, and felt a rush of relief when she twined her fingers around mine. "I thought Mister Smith had taken care of witnesses to the creature's attack," she added.

"Perhaps Harold Owston didn't want to be taken care of," I replied. Then, tentatively, "Jo?"

"Hmm?" She looked at me, her face shadowed by the purpling swelling.

"There weren't—there weren't village men at the Hall, were there? With Edward Masterson?"

She shook her head and promptly winced. "Ow. No, he never took on local men, he didn't trust them."

I nodded heavily. The angry looks some of the villagers had given us—oh, I wanted to put it down to Edward Masterson's influence, but it seemed they had formed their own unfavorable opinions.

Jo was still pushing at her nose, making little noises as she did so. "Is it very bad?" I asked.

"I've had worse," she muttered, then amended, "I think it's just swollen."

And that was all. She leaned back with another sigh, her

expression somber. I thought to speak, to further smooth over what had happened, but I realized I did not want to. I told myself it was because I was angry at her for letting Harold Owston make a spectacle of us and ruining any chance at further inquiries. But in truth, it was because I did not want to think on her question, and our complicity in the Mastersons' violence.

We rode in silence back to the house, and the daunting task of accelerating our removal to Medby. When we reached the drive, Jo was out of the carriage before I could speak, and I stayed to help Mr. Simmons unhitch the horses.

CHAPTER III

The Last Night

When I came inside, I found my father presiding over a laden table, for Mrs. Simmons had served dinner despite our absence. He beckoned me in, settling for waving as words so often failed him now. Beside him, Jo was sitting with a pleasant expression, holding a compress to her nose and working her fork around it. My father's smile was infectious, and despite my worries I smiled in return.

"Simmons," he said, holding up a clipping.

"From this morning's dispatch," Jo clarified as I took the paper. It detailed recent tensions with the French, including shipping losses in the North Sea. The foreboding tone, the dire predictions—I had to force myself to take some food.

"England needs us, sir," Jo continued. "Thomas Masterson has to be stopped before he provokes us to outright war." She smiled at my father, and his smile broadened in return. In contrast to Mrs. Simmons, my father had taken to Jo at once, despite having first made her acquaintance as Mr. Chase. I did not know what, exactly, he thought of her, as lengthy conversation was now impossible for him. But she could always rouse a smile from him, and sometimes even a belly-laugh. When had my father last laughed so? I was unable to recall a single time, at least since my mother died.

"Traitor?" my father inquired as he took a second helping of meat.

"Or perhaps just playing the odds," Jo said, pouring herself a large glass of burgundy. "I suspect Thomas Masterson's first loyalty is to money, rather than a particular king."

"Brute," my father said cheerfully. He pointed at her nose, looking at me. "Your doing?"

"Certainly not," I replied, but he only chuckled as he began eating, and not for the first time I wondered if the Fitzroys' attack had addled his wits in more ways than just his speech. That he was sitting here dining with us was nothing short of a miracle, but he was not the man I knew.

"Caroline," Jo drawled, "favors an instinctive hook. A pretty piece of fist-work, sir; you'd be proud to see it."

I gave her what I hoped was a withering look. I had told my father that Mr. Windham was tutoring me; I had not told him in exactly what subjects.

"Family trait," my father said around a mouthful. He jabbed his own fist in the air, nearly striking a candlestick. "For husbands," he added with another chuckle.

And there it was: *husband*. After all that had happened, my father still believed I should marry. His greatest objection to Medby had been that if I was posing as Jo's wife, I could not also meet potential suitors. And I, coward that I was, had parried by saying my duty was to the Crown first, when I should have stated plainly that the very thought of marriage to a man made me feel ill.

I snuck a glance at Jo. Her own good humor had evaporated. She was poking forcefully at her darkening bruises and it felt as if that finger was poking me.

A cough came from the door. "From Mister Windham," Mr. Simmons said, handing me a sealed letter. "A boy brought it from the village."

Jo's poking slowed as she watched me prise it open. I read it through, every word setting my nerves alight, then handed it to her.

Misses Chase and Daniels—

I will be brief, as I hope to start for London at once. Our visitor was indeed French, but he understood the locals' slang remarkably well, and seemed to know the coastline intimately. When he returned from the bay, he sent several letters and made immediate arrangements to 'tour the coast on his way to London.' I can only surmise that he apprised his masters of some validity to Thomas Masterson's threats, and is now on his way to Medby.

I have been advised that His Majesty does not want to give credence to rumors put about by a Northern merchant, especially in the wake of our recent troubles in Scotland. But Smith already has a man in Medby who will contact you as soon as you arrive. His name is Captain Herbert. I do not yet know the extent of my role in Grimsby, but if possible, I will hasten to join you, if for nothing else than to ensure Miss Daniels does not become distracted.

Yrs sincerely
R. Windham

"We should pack tonight," I said when Jo finished reading. "I will speak to Missus Simmons, to figure out how best to organize ourselves."

Jo simply nodded, and I excused myself and went out into the hall. Once there, I suddenly found myself with a tight throat and tears stinging my eyes. The house—my *home*, in all its familiarity, and suddenly we were to leave it—! I could not put words to all I felt, a jumble of grief and fear and a kind of reckless joy, like a bird about to flee its cage. It was some time before I mastered myself enough to make my way to the kitchen.

I was intent on assessing the food, the laundry, how quickly we could close the house … but the sight of the kitchen brought me up short. A cold supper was already assembled for the evening and hampers were packed for our journey. The pantry stores had been divided and labelled, some for storage, some to be given away. So startled was I, it took me a moment to see that Mrs. Simmons' apron was absent from its customary hook. When I turned around, she was standing in the doorway behind me, a large satchel in her hand.

"I'm giving my notice," she said.

It was as if she were speaking in a foreign language. I could only stare at her. "What?" I finally managed.

"I am giving my notice," she repeated. Her eyes were glistening. "I do not know Mister Simmons' mind, but I know my own. I'm going to my sister's. There is a cold supper ready—"

"You're leaving us?" I could not keep the astonishment from my voice. "But darling, what is the matter? Have I forgotten something, or—"

"I cannot countenance it," she burst out. "It's not right, Miss, it's not right. Bad enough that she fooled us all, coming here acting like a man, but now you would risk your poor father?" Her voice was trembling. "She's—she's *unnatural*. Everything about her is unwomanly and deceitful. I thought you would come to your senses, I thought you would make her leave and take her nonsense with her. Instead, you're following her down the same path."

At the last she clapped her hand over her mouth. Tears were spilling from her eyes, as they were from mine. Every word felt a blow, provoking the most chaotic, terrible feelings. I had never known a time in my life without her; I had never felt so betrayed.

When at last I was able to speak I said, "Miss Chase saved *my life*, Missus Simmons. She saved my life from an evil you cannot imagine, an evil that murdered your niece. If you had seen what I saw, you would not condemn my behavior now, you would encourage it."

At the mention of poor Emily she flinched, but her mouth hardened into a grim line. "I have never doubted that what you saw was horrible," she said. "What I doubt, Miss, is that you must continue to be involved. His Majesty has soldiers, munitions, learned men all at his disposal. Why does he need *you*?" Before I could speak she pressed, "Because, in truth, he does not; *she* does. She wants a companion for her perversities and she has chosen you. I beg of you, send her away now, before it is too late."

I hesitated then. Not in my answer, but in how to say it. Mrs. Simmons had been my mother in many ways, yet I could not explain to her all that was in my heart. So I simply answered, "No."

The word made her bow her head as she stifled a sob. "Even if it means hurting your father?" she asked in a shuddering voice.

"Hurting him? We are bringing him in order to care for him!" I cried. "We have a letter of introduction for one of the finest physicians in England—"

"That is not what I meant," she cut in, "and you know it, Miss. That trick hasn't worked since you were clinging to my apron. You are going to go to Medby to pretend to be *married*, pretend to be a common clerk's wife with that *person*. Your father thinks it a little adventure, and you'll be back in time for the Christmas assemblies—"

"My father," I interrupted coolly, "is aware of what is at stake. If he spoke of assemblies I suspect it was to assuage your concerns. Or have you forgotten that I have been given this role by the Crown? I do not second-guess His Majesty, as you seem comfortable doing—"

"If you think that man Smith truly has His Majesty's ear, then you're a bigger fool than I thought," Mrs. Simmons interrupted in turn.

We glared at each other, each of us panting as if we had come to blows. Then Mrs. Simmons' expression softened. "I know it's not my place to speak so," she said, a sob in her voice. "But can't you see how you debase yourself?" She dabbed at her eyes. "Your poor mother," she whispered. "I thank God she did not live to see this."

To invoke my mother now, on this last day—I could stand no more. "I will fetch your wages," I said in as flat a voice as I could manage. "And, of course, if you need a recommendation we will be happy to provide it."

My words made her flinch, but I took no pleasure in it. At some point I had begun weeping outright; we were both weeping. She gave me an exaggerated curtsey, then went to the door, only to pause once more.

"If you will give no thought to yourself," she said in a low voice, "then I beg you to think of your father. Go, if you must, but let him stay here. He does not have the strength for this, and surely … surely you can let him have his hopes, that he will be a grandfather one day."

With that, she turned and walked out of the kitchen, shutting the door behind her. A woman who I had known all my life, who had cared for me like a mother. I clapped a hand over my mouth lest anyone hear my sobbing.

I thought, then, to give it all up. To send Jo away, to return to my small, familiar life. If I went to Medby tomorrow, there would be no turning back.

But, in truth, it was already too late. I had tasted too much this year: too much freedom, too much risk, too much … oh, there was a memory of a kiss in darkness that would haunt me forever if I did not go. Life had come to my door and I would not, I *could* not, refuse to answer.

Instead, I set about my tasks. My chest ached and stung, as if some long-hidden wound had been touched by air. Still

I found myself listening for Mrs. Simmons' step in the hall. But when someone at last came it was not Mrs. Simmons but her husband, looking abashed.

"I—I've seen Jane off," he said, clearly choosing his words with care. "Albert, her sister's boy, he's offered to close up the house. So we can leave tomorrow if you like."

My throat was pin-tight. I could only nod.

"Miss," he continued in the same careful manner, "if you would rather hire someone else—"

"No!" I cried, then swallowed hard. "I—I do not wish to hire anyone," I said. Everything sounded as if I were underwater, distant and echoing. "But I do not wish to separate you two. I could not bear it if I was the cause of any discord."

He broke into a relieved smile. "Now, Miss. Don't you worry about us," he said reassuringly. "You've got enough to worry about. Just make sure you've packed everything you want to bring and Albert will see to the rest. All right?"

"All right," I said thickly, trying to smile.

He seemed about to speak, hesitated, then said in the same reassuring tone, "She'll come around, Miss. You'll see." Before I could reply, he withdrew, leaving me alone in the dim, echoing kitchen. As much as I wanted to believe him, I suspected the gulf between us could only be repaired by repudiating my very heart; that this was the cost of being true to myself. The understanding sat cold and heavy in my stomach.

It was late when I arrived at some semblance of readiness for our departure: all the clothes packed, the valuables locked away, a list of instructions written up for Albert. I thought, again, of how much we depended on the Simmonses, how little would be possible without them.

My father had long since retired. Jo, I knew, had been as busy as I, between packing and composing letters that might plausibly account for our early arrival in Medby. Mr. Simmons, I had last seen heading for the stables.

I moved through the house, checking room by room, extinguishing lights and testing the window bolts as I went. In the past, one of the Simmonses would have made this circuit. It felt strangely final to be undertaking the task myself. My entire life had been spent between these walls. Would I ever see it again? And if I did not, would I look back in regret upon this moment?

In my father's study, I paused, letting the candlelight play over the spines, the cracking leather of the chairs. In a way I had already lost the home I knew, first through my mother's passing and now with my father's injury. He no longer immersed himself in reading, for he complained of headache after a few minutes. He could no longer walk to the village, and in the cold weather, few came to visit. To see his once-garrulous self so reduced was sometimes more than I could bear.

I started to extinguish the candles when I heard a quick step down the stairs. For a moment, I thought it was Mrs. Simmons returned, but instead Jo came into the room. She was wearing an old banyan, a familiar garment from her restless mornings. Now, however, she looked as tired as I felt. In one hand she held a large pair of shears, and in the other she carried a candlestick.

"You're still awake?" She frowned as she came forward. "Tell me you don't have more to do."

"I was just putting out the candles," I said.

Jo put the candlestick down on a table and closed the door. "Caroline … I saw Missus Simmons leave, and heard some of her conversation with Mister Simmons. I'm so sorry." She shook her head as I started to speak. "I should have come to you earlier, only I, I was afraid you might not want to go—"

"Stop it," I snapped, then softened my voice. "I think it is less that she is upset by you, and more that she is at last truly seeing me—? Or perhaps it is that I am no longer able to dissemble …"

She crossed the room in a few swift steps and hugged me. The feel of her, the smell of her—oh! Here was what I had been missing these long days, and this the longest of them all. Just the sensation of her holding me made everything feel *possible*, when before all had seemed hopeless.

"Why are you still awake?" I said into her neck.

"I was looking for a second mirror." She drew back and tugged at her unpinned brown hair. "It's time," she said. "Only I thought I would make a better job of it with two mirrors."

It took my weary mind a moment to piece together what she was saying. We had talked about her appearance, should any of Edward Masterson's men have fled to Thomas. Young Mr. Chase would be swiftly recognized; but an older, bewigged, and bespectacled Mr. Read might pass as just another clerk.

I tucked a loose lock of hair behind her ear, relishing the softness. It would grow back, I told myself. I would insist upon it.

That we might not live to have that argument, I did not think on.

"I'll do it," I said, angling my head. "Sit."

She pressed the shears in my hand and sat in one of the armchairs, legs crossed like a man, fluffing her tangled hair over her shoulders. I brought the candlestick close, then two others. The shears were old but gleaming and sharp—Mrs. Simmons always took care of her tools. I combed out Jo's hair with my fingers, massaging out tangles, pulling out a stray piece of leaf from goodness knew where. It was late, so late; it was also the first time since she had come back to me that we were truly alone. Her head rolled back, her mouth curving into a smile. I leaned over and let my lips brush hers.

"Practice," I whispered.

She responded by sliding her hand around my head and drawing me closer. Her kiss was like tasting something forbidden. I had a sudden vision of my father walking in on us and pulled upright, but there was nothing save the looming shadows held at bay by the fragile, fluttering lights.

"Do your worst, Missus Read," she said, her eyes half-lidded.

I took a handful of her hair and cut it. The sound of the shears was loud in the silence. Again and again I cut, letting her locks fall to the floor like so many wilted blossoms. The shears were heavy in my hand, her hair twisted every which way as the blades came down, yet it was the work of a few moments to cut away the mass. Before she could speak, I began again, sliding my fingers against her head and resting the blades against them as I cut. Beneath my hand, I felt every curve and rise of her skull; watched with fascination the glimpses of the paler skin of her scalp. When I finished, I was breathing hard. The eyes that met mine were full of emotion.

Slowly, Jo rose and angled her head to see herself in the reflection of a polished vase. She seemed slighter, her bruised nose more vivid; yet somehow the combined effect made her appear more substantial. Although I mourned the soft waves littering the floor, I knew instinctively that she was more herself.

"Thank you," she said.

In response, I took her hand. Her fingers promptly entwined with mine, her palm warm and snug against my own. Together we moved around the room, pushing the hair into a neater pile, then slowly extinguishing all but the one candle that Jo held before us like a beacon. Together we left, Jo waiting while I closed the study door noiselessly, and slid our arms around each other as we ascended the stairs. Tomorrow our pretense would begin. *Practice*, I had said, only this did not feel like practice but a summation. At the door to my room she kissed me and I kissed her, we kissed, and when she planted a last soft kiss against my lower lip, it seemed a promise. I was senseless as I walked to my own bed. I never knew if she lingered at the door or simply went to her own room, for I was asleep the moment my head touched the pillow.

—and for the first time since the spring, I dreamed of a blood-red sea parting to reveal that coiling, writhing black form as it opened its tentacles in a ghastly embrace. Only this time, it was not I tumbling towards its open maw but Jo, and I helpless to do anything but watch.

CHAPTER IV

Traveling

We made quite a picture in our dilapidated carriage, our possessions strapped higgledy-piggledy on the top and back, and Jo with her swollen nose. Mr. Simmons drove while we three practiced our stories: Jo and I were recently married, but my father's illness required both better employment and the sea air. Mr. Simmons had served my father in the army and stayed on despite our declining fortunes. None of which was an outright lie.

I wore an old wool dress and a cloak I had purchased from one of the Simmonses' many relatives. Jo was wearing a serviceable suit, appropriate for an educated man seeking to better his circumstances. For my father, we had delved into the attic and found his older, slightly motheaten clothes, the better to convey a gentleman on hard times. He seemed pleased with his new role and took to ordering twopenny while we changed horses. Watching him, I wondered at Mrs. Simmons' presentation of his health—unless, in speaking of my father's discomfort, was she describing her own unease?

As the day wore on, though, he began to complain, first of the poor roads, then the cold—and this despite the blankets and heated bricks that kept us snug. I still did not know the true extent of his lingering injuries from the spring. He never quantified his complaints of aches and stiffness, though I knew he was more explicit with Mr. Simmons. When he groaned aloud during a particularly rutted stretch of road, Jo took my hand under the lap blanket. One glance told me she was as concerned as I.

"At the next inn," she murmured in my ear, "perhaps we should speak with Mister Simmons? We may want to put up for the night earlier than planned. What do you think?"

Her words brought into sharp relief my confrontation with Mrs. Simmons. So many of my conversations with Jo were true exchanges: what did I think? Did I agree with her, or did I foresee problems? What would be my suggestion? For years I had tended my quota of household duties and left the rest to Mrs. Simmons. Over the past weeks, however, I had discovered that I held opinions on a great many things.

"I agree," I replied now. "Though I think if he eats, and we can perhaps cushion him better, he might bear a little more. But Mister Simmons knows his health better than anyone—even that damn surgeon."

My language made her smile. "Think on him no more," she said, squeezing my hand again. "We have a better man awaiting us in Medby. Doctor Denham is one of the finest physicians in England."

At last we rocked and wobbled into the tamped center of a village. It would have been a pretty green in summertime; now, with winter arriving, it was a muddy patch laced with brown grass and melted frost. My father peered blearily out of the window. "Famished," he declared.

Jo and I exchanged a look. "I shall fetch you something," I said. "Do you want to walk a little? The air is close in here."

At that moment, Mr. Simmons opened the door and my father recoiled from the chill wind. "I do not," he retorted with such vigor, my heart swelled. How many invalids would have made it this far? Even as he huddled under the blanket, he kept peering about, watching the people walking to and fro, the bustling shops with their doors ringing merrily.

"Is there anything special you'd like, Mister Daniels?" Jo asked as she wiggled out of the carriage.

He gave me a squinty-eyed look, then leaned over and whispered loudly, "Cream buns."

"You've had a great many cream buns lately, thanks to Missus Simmons," I admonished him. When he looked crestfallen, however, I amended, "but I think we can make an exception."

"I'll see about the horses," Mr. Simmons said as he helped me out.

"Do you need a cream bun as well?" I asked.

He grinned. "I'd rather have ale, but that can wait until we're in for the night."

"Speaking of," Jo began in a low voice.

"We've not got much further," Mr. Simmons said as he closed the door. "It's the hip bothering him, I'm sure. I'll see what I can do about making him more comfortable. But I know he'll be disappointed if we stop early on account of him."

Reassured, I let Jo take my arm, as gentlemanly as any husband, and took up my basket. The village was lively, the sky bright despite the scuttling gray clouds. Chill air stung my cheeks and raised a flush in Jo's. As we crossed the muddy green together, I wished I had thought to wear my pattens—

And then we both stopped in astonishment.

Tacked to a tree before us was a broadside, the ink dark and fresh. At the bottom was a symbol, like a sun with undulating rays, that we both knew all too well. An innocuous shape, unless you knew it showed the maw of an unholy monster just before it consumed you. The same symbol had been tattooed on Edward Masterson, and burned on the crates of his brother's goods.

Above the image, in large type, were the words TO ALL GOOD ENGLISHMEN, followed by a brief paragraph:

The great and holy nation of ENGLAND is beset on all sides, but God has heard Our Prayers. Subscriptions in support of the ship LEVIATHAN will be used to protect our sovereign waters. Monies and inquiries to T. Masterson, Importer, Medby. May God Protect Us from the French menace.

"A ship called *Leviathan*? But that's what he called—"

Jo squeezed my arm and I silenced. She nudged me forward, keeping a bland smile on her face. "Too many to tell if we're being watched," she said, her lips barely moving.

We bought bread, cheese, and cream buns for the road, and on our way back to the carriage, Jo gallantly bought me a silk flower to pin to my cloak. We paused by the broadside while she pinned it on, and in the guise of holding my head away I reviewed it once more, in case we had missed any detail.

We made our way back to the carriage only to find Mr.

Simmons had ensconced my father in the warmth of the inn while he saw to the horses. He was nursing a glass of beer in a corner, but his eyes lit up as Jo unwrapped a cream bun, which he promptly devoured with enthusiasm.

"Glad I came," he said, patting my hand. "Glad."

"We are glad to have you, Mister Daniels," Jo put in with a smile.

My father started to speak but struggled for the words. At last, he touched his hat. "Mister Read," he said with a wink.

When the landlord came to see to us, Jo asked lightly, "There is a curious notice on the tree outside. What does it mean?" At his confusion she continued, "Something about the French, and 'All Good Englishmen'?"

He grinned slyly at the latter. "Ah yes, the Yorkshire Navy! Aye, seems some rich ass down in Medby fancies he can get a subscription to support his privateering. Though, some say it's Jacobites again, and others say there's no ship at all, that it's actually the Biblical beast sailing up and down the coast. Bloody idiots," he added, as if that explained everything.

"Would that I had the coin to indulge such nonsense," Jo said.

"Ah, well, that seems to be one thing young Masterson has plenty of—coin." The landlord sucked his teeth. "I told his fellows, you'll not be spreading that drivel in my house. He's got the real Navy sniffing around."

"His fellows—here?" I looked around in feigned alarm. "Surely there are no such madmen nearby!"

"Now, don't you worry, miss," the landlord said. "It was this past summer they were nosing around here, looking for recruits." He pointed at the door. "Look! Seems your man is ready for you now."

Mr. Simmons beckoned us from the doorway, and soon we were once again snug and on our way, this time with the added benefit of extra bricks and a cushion for my father's hip. When we were beyond the village limits, my father suddenly spoke. "Jacobites," he said, nodding at me.

At Jo's confused look, I explained. "For a few years, there were broadsides and pamphlets everywhere. Full of lies to encourage people to join the Pretender's army. It swayed quite a few. He may be looking to exploit that sentiment."

"There's nothing a man likes more than to feel he belongs to something," Jo said.

There was an odd note in her voice, but I could not think how to respond, and the conversation swiftly changed to the rest of our journey. Still, I mused upon her words for some time.

It was late when we reached our destination for the night, later still when we had sorted our things, eaten supper, and got my father settled. When I left him, I was weary in my very bones. Who would think that just sitting could be so tiring?

Thus, I had not given a moment's thought to our room arrangements until I entered and found Jo undressing. I had known this moment was coming. At times it had seemed a light at the end of a long, dark road. Yet now that it had arrived, I was overcome with shyness.

When she looked at me, however, it was with the same trepidation in her own face. "Caroline," she said, then stopped, then began again. "That is—I know this is sudden, and I—when I suggested this, this ploy … I never had any expectations."

Her eyes were everywhere but my face, yet I could not stop gazing at her. How her shorn hair caught the candlelight, how a thin trail of smoke from the stove curled around her face. Her hands were twisting her waistcoat buttons.

"I can sleep in the chair," she continued. "It makes no odds to me. Or I can sleep in the carriage. God knows I've slept rougher."

Impulsively, I reached forward, laying my hands over hers to still them. In her belly was a fluttering pulse, rabbit-fast.

"I confess I am unclear as to my own expectations," I said. My voice was trembling but I made no attempt to hide it. "But I know I don't want you to go."

Her grey eyes finally met mine. Her lips parted but she did not speak.

"Could we not—" I took a breath. "Could we not just rest? Together? I am so very, very tired … dear God, Jo, I just want to sleep, in a bed, with you. Could we not just do that?"

She smiled then, and with exaggerated care took my hand in hers and raised it to her lips. "As you wish, Missus Read," she whispered.

I flushed at her words and began unbuttoning her waistcoat, careful to untwist the buttons she had nearly wrenched off. She began unpinning my bodice in turn, and as she undid my skirts, I carefully unbuttoned her breeches with trembling fingers.

We each shucked off our clothes like children. Our eyes met and we began giggling, almost helplessly, shaking with small rushes of relieved laughter. She unlaced my stays and I unlaced her jumps and we each flung them off with a little joyous cry. Jo dashed to the bed and I followed as quickly, wiggling next to her as we mock-wrestled for the coverlet, a tangle of limbs and arms and smothering pillows until at last, gasping, we twined together in the warmth.

It was as if her touch was a strong drink, so swiftly did I feel my body relax into a drowsy softness that was more comforting, more *right*, than any embrace I had ever known.

Her lips pressed against my hair and I breathed her in, listening to the rhythm of her breath and the soft patter of her heart and the fall of the dwindling coals and oh it was it was

Wonderful.

PART II

Medby

CHAPTER V

Arrivals

In this way we traveled to Medby. At each stop in our journey, we saw more broadsides and heard more stories of something large sailing along the coast at night. "As if he took the beast on a tour," Jo remarked after the third such conversation. Whatever Thomas Masterson's intent, the effect of such displays was clear: there was a great deal of angry talk about the French and taking our own back; there were also more quiet mutterings that God Himself had sent a clear mark of favor for Masterson's cause.

Yet, I wondered at his ultimate purpose. Without clear evidence of the power he wielded, how would he command a price for his services? While I dreaded a repeat of the beast's terrifying attack, I could not see any monarch paying for rumors.

Or so I told Jo, as we snuggled in bed. "I have wondered as well," she said. "The damage from last spring is still visible, but it could have been caused by men as easily as the monster. Instead, he has the whole coastline talking of revenge and shadows: why? There must be another reason."

But try as we might, we could not think of one, and our arrival in Medby only underscored our ignorance.

What can I say about cresting that last hill and seeing Medby for the first time? Crowded and populous, our first glimpse was of a town crammed on rocky hillsides leading down to a bay with a broad, curving beach, framed by a harbor wall and so thronged with masts it seemed impossible for any to move. I was not a complete stranger to either towns or cities, but the crowds of people, the boisterous marketplace, the noise—it startled me, and I did not at first sense the tension in the air. Everywhere were men from all walks of life who seemed neither idle nor purposeful, but somehow *waiting*. They watched passersby with sharp eyes and exchanged brief words with one another. From my lessons with Mr. Windham, even I could see the readiness in their postures. It would take little to provoke them.

We had to cross the town to reach our lodging, following a circuitous route to avoid the steep streets leading down to the bay, and we soon understood what was agitating the populace. Chalked onto walls and fences were phrases in violent language, sometimes with crude drawings, all against the French. Elsewhere, they had inscribed *Remember the Othello* and *Remember the Minerva*. As we reached the town center, there were more signs of upheaval: not one but three blackened effigies, still smoldering.

A man was handing out papers in an open square ringed by a large crowd. The tension was palpable. Mr. Simmons slowed us to nearly a crawl to get past the crowd, which allowed us to hear what was being said.

"One hundred good men," he bellowed, handing out paper after paper. "One hundred good men at the door tomorrow. The *Leviathan* sails by week's end, and by God, we'll show them just what the English can do."

Jo and I both gasped, though the sound was lost in the crowd's roar of approval. My father leaned out the window and gestured to a nearby man. "May I?" he asked, pointing to the paper.

The man passed it to him. "New to Medby?" he asked.

Jo nodded. "We heard a ship was lost," she said.

"Not lost," the man growled. "It was the God-damned French. And if our king has no stomach for it, we'll go to war without him."

My father handed the paper to Jo and I. One hundred men, and those who could not sail were invited to subscribe. Twenty noble families supported the cause. God Himself, the paper concluded, would guide them and protect England from the mercenary, Papist French.

At the bottom was an address and a name. *Thos. Masterson.*

When I started to speak, Jo pressed a finger to her lips, then touched her ear and pointed at the window: with so many standing close by, we might be heard. My father kept looking at the crowd, his fingers tapping. I realized he was counting.

"Too many," he finally murmured, sitting back in the carriage with a worried expression.

As we turned a corner, I looked back at the square. A thin plume of smoke rose in the air, and a moment later a straw figure in a blue jacket swung upwards—a crude effigy of a French soldier. Already the figure was bursting into flames.

It took some time, and many questions, for Mr. Simmons to find our little house. It was one of a row of tiny, grim cottages facing a street so narrow, we had to keep moving the carriage to let traffic by. The key was in a pot by the door, yet it barely turned from disuse; it took the combined efforts of Mr. Simmons turning and Jo pushing to force the door open. Inside, damp clung to the walls and the still-covered furnishings, and the cold air was stale. But it was home now, for better or worse, and I set myself to making the most of it.

Mr. Simmons took the carriage to the stables, Jo set about hunting for coal, and I settled my father in the front room where the weak sun gave some warmth. As I tucked the blankets around him he nodded at the shabby room. "Work," he said.

"We'll have it clean and cozy in no time," I assured him with more certainty than I felt. The more I looked around, the more I saw: peeling wallpaper, rodent droppings, drafts from all sides—

—then I realized the latter was Jo, who had opened the door and was now saying briskly, "Good afternoon!"

I joined her at the front door, smiling at the old woman on our step with a basket in her hands. She kept peering around Jo, who was leaning against the doorframe in just the right position to block her view.

"Dearest," Jo said, holding out her hand to me. "Come meet our neighbor. This is Missus Lambert. Missus Lambert, may I present my wife, Missus Read." Her eyes were crinkled up with mirth. "*Remarkable* timing; I was just going out as she was about to knock."

"It is lovely to meet you, Missus Lambert," I said, inclining my head.

"I was just finishing my baking and I thought you could do with some bread," she said, holding out the basket. I plucked it from her hands, further blocking her view. "Are you a sailor, then, Mister Read?"

"A mere accountant," Jo said. "I have hopes of a position with Mister Masterson's firm."

"Oh, you're working for Mister Masterson!" She clasped her hands to her bosom. "A most wonderful gentleman. So charming—especially with the ladies. You will not want to introduce him to your pretty wife."

"Missus Lambert!" I exclaimed.

"Now, now, we ladies can admit what's true, can't we? He's a fine figure of a man, Mister Masterson. They say he might even have a title soon—perhaps Lord Masterson?" She frowned then. "Can you be made a lord?"

"I don't see why not," Jo said. "If he's wealthy enough, that is."

"Oh, he's very rich," Mrs. Lambert said vaguely, rising on tiptoes. I glanced behind us and saw my father peeping around the corner. "And if he bests the French, they will have to reward him, I should think."

"Bests the French?" Jo sounded incredulous. I had to admire

her skill. "An importer against Louis's navy? Oh, do go on, Missus."

"But it's true!" She gestured at the houses behind her, beyond which lay the bay. "The *Leviathan* is a proper ship of war, and Mister Masterson says God sent him the idea in a dream."

Before we could reply, my father shuffled forward, his wig slightly askew. Jo and I each had to twist to let him through. He bowed so low, I thought he would topple over. Miraculously, his wig stayed in place.

"Dear lady," he said, but then words failed him.

"May I introduce my father," I put in. "Mister Theophilus Daniels. This is Missus Lambert, Father." I leaned over and added in a low voice, "He was injured earlier this year. We are hoping the sea air might prove a tonic."

"Oh, I see," Mrs. Lambert murmured. "How do you do," she said loudly, enunciating each word.

My father recoiled. "Not deaf," he said huffily, and I quickly took his arm.

"Let us go to the kitchen," I said, "and have some dinner." I smiled at Mrs. Lambert. "Forgive him, please," I added in a whisper. "He gets irritable when he hasn't eaten."

"Not at all. You should have seen my mister when he was famished, God rest his soul." She started forward. "I could help prepare something—"

"You are too kind," Jo said firmly, "but we are not even unpacked. Thank you for the basket, it is much appreciated. As soon as we've settled in we will be sure to repay your generosity."

Mrs. Lambert kept talking even as Jo worked the door closed and I steered my father into the kitchen where the stove was warming.

"Not deaf," he fumed.

"Of course you're not," I said. "Don't pay her any mind."

"Nosy old dear," Jo said from the doorway. "But she did give us a possible motive. Though, buying a ship, stoking anti-French rhetoric for months, and playing keeper to that beast seems a great deal of work just to become Lord Masterson."

"His brother was fanatical," I suggested. "Perhaps Thomas shares his beliefs."

"Perhaps." She frowned. "We need to look at that ship and possibly get word to Mister Smith—though we still have no word on this Captain Herbert."

But I was shaking my head. "First, we need to make this place habitable." I had managed to cobble together a plate for my father, who fell upon it with relish. "And eat something ourselves." The front door opened. "Ah! Here is Mister Simmons with more coal. Eat," I repeated when Jo shifted with impatience. "Eat and help me, and later we can look at ships, *husband*."

She joined my father at the table, though I caught a flash of her tongue sticking out at me. In truth, I was as impatient as she: a war with the French would mean devastation for thousands and I felt frantic to stop any such plotting. But I had my father to think of, and who knew what forces might be arrayed against us, and to what end?

CHAPTER VI

The Two Leviathans

It was well into evening by the time we finished dusting and airing the rooms, beating the coverlets and the rugs, and cleaning the kitchen. Although I had been bewildered by the small size of the cottage, I was quickly thankful there was that much less to clean. Still, we were quite cramped, and my father and Mr. Simmons were reduced to sharing a bed.

"It's all right, Miss," Mr. Simmons said after I apologized yet again. "I've slept worse, believe me. Besides," he lowered his voice, "I prefer to keep an eye on him. He's got a feverish look, I'm a little worried after that journey."

My father's complexion was indeed pale, and despite the chill in the house, sweat stood out upon his brow. "I will take him to that physician tomorrow," I said.

"You shouldn't trouble yourself. I can certainly—"

"We all have many things to do," I interrupted. "Including you writing to your good wife. We shall see how the day progresses," I amended at his frown, "but I would like to be the one to take him, if possible."

Though I braced for disagreement, he merely said, "Take care on your walk tonight, Miss."

"Oh?"

"It's a port town," he said. "Bigger than what you're used to. The lads might be rowdy and there's probably a curfew. Just take care."

"We'll take care," Jo put in. She already had her greatcoat on and was holding out my cloak. As she arranged it over my shoulders, I felt a familiar weight in the pocket: the little knife she had given me when I first began my lessons. She had a pistol under her coat and I knew the bump at the top of her boot to be the end of another knife.

"Do you want a pistol as well?" she whispered.

I considered. "No, I think one between us should suffice," I replied, keeping my voice low. "It is just a stroll, after all."

We took our leave of my father and Mr. Simmons and stepped out into the cold, still night air. We set out for the bay, stepping carefully down the steep paths, clutching each other's hand as we hit patches of ice on the cobblestones. Lights were on in the cottages around us, and we heard noises even through the closed and shuttered windows: laughter, singing, arguing. Somewhere, crockery smashed and a cat yowled. As we crossed one street, stepping over the long lines of rope laid out to dry, a stooped figure stumbled into the road. He nearly fell over, but with a sideways lurch righted himself and began shuffling away. From an open doorway, a woman bellowed out, "And good riddance!" with such rage in her voice that I flinched.

"They're both drunk," Jo said soothingly. "Let's just hope he doesn't freeze to death."

I said nothing, only pressed closer to her. In our village, a drunk like Harold Owston was an exceptional circumstance.

But I had heard stories about the larger port towns and I had glimpsed the nighttime antics of Londoners. I wished I had that second pistol, but there was nothing for it now.

We were in sight of the bay for several steps before I looked up, and when I did so, the sight stopped me short. In the bright moonlight, the bay was thronging with boats, large and small, their masts jumbled together against the stars …

But the farthest of them all overshadowed the rest, its hulking form like an inkblot atop the horizon.

"What is it?" I whispered.

"It's a frigate," Jo breathed. "He's bought himself a bloody frigate."

"It may not be his—"

"It's the only boat that could be described as a warship." She tugged on my hand. "Let's see if we can get a better look."

Two sharp turns through a ginnel and we were at the water's edge at last. Men were milling about in small groups, huddled against the cold; alehouses, inns, and shipping offices alike were still open despite the hour. Life at the waterfront paid little heed to curfews—if, indeed, there was one. A man crashed into us, nearly knocking me off my feet in a cloud of liquor, and stumbled on; somewhere at the far end was a circle of shouting men and two fellows engaged in fisticuffs.

"Sailors," Jo said, as if that explained everything. She tucked my arm in hers and we began to stroll along the narrow strip of paved walkway. To our left were the storefronts, to our right the broad beach that led to the bay, dotted with boats in various states of repair.

My eyes were drawn, however, not to the bay or its ominous resident, but to the glowing windows we were passing. The singing, the shouting, the smoke rising from the cracked, steam-covered glass—it was at once a ridiculous, drunken spectacle and yet somehow *alive*. Uncouth, Mrs. Simmons would have called such men and meant it an insult, but now I thought it simply a truth: they were uncouth in that they acted as they pleased, without thought of propriety or consequences. What would I do, if I acted on my desires? I looked at Jo's profile in the darkness—

—then I stopped and seized her to me, crushing her mouth with my own, all my pent-up emotions finding some release at last.

She made a choking noise, then returned my passionate embrace. Her hands holding me, stroking, and, oh, that I could have found us a bed there and then …

At last we moved apart, gasping. She started to speak, only to be drowned out by sudden bellowing from the nearest alehouse:

Here's a health to our Tom and a lasting peace,
To faction an end, to wealth increase;
Come, let us drink it while we have breath,
For there's no drinking after death,
And he that will this health deny,
Down among the dead men,
Down among the dead men,
Down, down, down, down,
Down among the dead men let him lie.

"They are so *free*," I blurted out. "They can do whatever they wish."

"Including dying miserable and alone," Jo said. As I fell silent her hands found mine. "There was a time in my life when all I craved was that freedom, but it can be a lonely thing, Caroline." Her voice was somber. "People can circumscribe you, but they also give you a reason to live."

"Yes, but ..." I struggled to find the words. "When I am home, even now? I feel as if I must be my father's Caroline, or the little girl everyone knew. And yet, I want to be this Caroline, *your* Caroline—"

"Not mine," she cut in. "Just be Caroline."

I could say nothing for the sudden lump in my throat; I could only hold her hands tight, tight.

"I told you when I first came back," she continued. "I wanted to know *you* better, whether or not you might return my affections." She smiled warmly. "Though now, after that kiss? Bloody hell, darling. A few more such and you'll never be rid of me."

My face was burning. I was thankful for the darkness. "Say that again," I whispered.

"Bloody hell," she repeated, grinning.

"Not that." I gave her arm a little slap. "Don't tease me, not now."

Her expression softened then as she kissed me once more, saying in deed all that we could not say in words. And we might have stayed in that embrace forever, but a man cleared his throat behind us and we whirled about, blushing like errant children. "Too cheap to pay for the room as well?" he asked.

"How dare you," I said hotly. "We're married!"

"Of course you are," he drawled. He wore the livery of a servant, but finely cut, the white of his stock vivid against his brown skin. Too, he seemed more solid than anyone we had yet seen, and I suspected he would have given Mr. Windham a challenge. "Take your business elsewhere, Madame," he continued. "Mister Masterson doesn't like molls dirtying up his frontage."

At the name I looked up, and indeed we were standing before a large building with a single lantern burning over the door. In the dim light, I could just make out *Thos. Masterson & Co.* inscribed in dull gold paint.

"That's enough," Jo snapped, stepping before me. "That's my wife you're speaking to, *sir*. I am Joseph Read and I am expected at Mister Masterson's establishment as his newest clerk. I was showing my wife the ships in the moonlight."

"A clerk *and* a poet," the man replied derisively. "Well, if you are who you say you are, Mister Read, then I am Francis Morrow, and you're going to be seeing a lot of me." He angled his head. "They'll start ringing for curfew soon. I suggest you be on your way, unless you want to explain yourselves to the watchman."

"Good advice," Jo said, taking my arm as she touched her hat. "I thank you for it, Mister Morrow."

The *Mister* made him squint, but he merely gestured us inland. "So, what," Jo purred when we were out of earshot, "is Thomas Masterson hiding in his offices, that he pays to have them guarded at night?"

"He thought I was a whore," I whispered furiously. "A

whore! This is my second-best wool dress!"

"To be fair, Caroline," Jo whispered back, "the only women out at this hour are grandmothers and whores, and you're not quite old enough for the former."

I scowled at her, at the moonlight, at the waterfront receding behind us. "What do you think he's hiding in there?"

"If he's anything like his brother, I'm not sure I want to know," Jo said, "but I'm going to find out."

"Oh." It struck me that the list of items warranting a guard of Mr. Morrow's stature were few and unpleasant. Edward Masterson had hidden munitions and the corpses of women in Harkworth Hall. Now his brother had lured the beast down to these waters—with what bait?

But I could not ask, for I was breathless. The walk down had been precarious, but the walk up was exhausting. How was it that people lived on such steep inclines? Our feet passed upper-story windows of houses seemingly cut into the earth, their small gardens at a level with their roofs. I was suddenly terribly homesick. The journey today, the mob, Mr. Morrow, and above all, that massive ship in the harbor made our task seem far more than two women could accomplish. *Why you*, Mrs. Simmons had asked, and I realized I had no answer.

As if in response to my thoughts, the sound came.

It was a long, sustained wail, a single plaintive note that filled the night around us, echoing off the stone walls, sinking into our very bones. The waterfront fell quiet, as if all of Medby were listening to the lingering sound. Instinctively, Jo and I pressed together. The bay behind us was still, but I felt certain that the sound came from the black horizon.

"Leviathan," I breathed.

Jo slid her arms around me. My heart was aching, aching in ways I had no words for.

"We'll win through," she said, her voice low and urgent. "We will survive this, Caroline."

I nodded, but I did not trust myself to speak. With a last look at the bay she tucked my hand under her arm once more, and we walked back to our house in silence.

CHAPTER VII

Diagnosis

It was to a grey, icy morning that I saw Jo off, checking the height of her cravat, the faint touches of soot she had used to artfully darken beneath her eyes. With her wig, spectacles, and worn suit, she looked nothing like the brash Mr. Chase who had come to my house last spring. She looked like a man struggling to maintain respectability.

"Slightly desperate?" she asked as I surveyed her.

"Feeling the pinch, as Missus Simmons would say," I confirmed.

"Ten years older," Mr. Simmons agreed from the kitchen, where he was wiping dishes. "And the kind of fellow who might turn a blind eye for a few bob."

"Let us pray for petty crime, then," Jo said, "that we can clap him in irons before that ship sails."

"Because starting a war isn't enough?" Mr. Simmons shook his head. "Believe me, he's made Medby a powder keg."

I made a small noise of dismay; Jo scowled at Mr. Simmons. "Then let's hope nothing sparks," she snapped, and with a swift kiss on my lips, stormed out the door.

It was only when I turned and saw Mr. Simmons' odd expression that I realized what she had done. My face flared hot. “I must be off as well,” I said before he could speak. “Father’s appointment.” And with that poor excuse, I nearly ran up the stairs.

“Your father is ready now.”

Dr. Denham gestured me into his office. Inside, my father was seated in a chair, fumbling with his cravat. Fresh blood sat in a bowl on a side table. Still, my father smiled at me as I knelt by his side to tie his cravat for him.

“Your father has recovered remarkably well from the attack you described, Missus Read,” Dr. Denham said as soon as I was seated. “That he can walk at all is a miracle.”

“You say ‘recovered,’” I said. “Surely there is more to be done for him?”

“For the hip, no.” The doctor shrugged. “I am sorry, Missus Read. The damage is permanent now, though I do not mean this as a slight against my colleague. He handled the injury well enough. As for your father’s speech?” He leaned back, steepling his fingers. “The brain is an unknown, but most delicate instrument. This problem is one I have not seen before. Stuttering, substituting words: these are more common results. Your father can articulate the correct words, but he has difficulty uttering them all.” He held up a paper and read, “‘It is as if I forget *how* to speak *as* I speak.’ In writing, you see, he is more capable of expression, though it takes him some time to form the words.”

I stared at the page he held out to me, inscribed with what

looked like a terrible imitation of my father's handwriting. The letters wobbled, sometimes to the point of illegibility. But the sentence was more than he had uttered in months, and the realization made me heartsick.

"I never thought …" Tears welled in my eyes as I turned to my father. "I never thought to have you write."

He smiled again as he handed me his handkerchief. "Surprised me," he said.

Dr. Denham leaned forward, writing as he spoke. "I understand from Mister Smith that you are here at his behest, and I know better than to inquire further. But should time and finances permit, I have a friend who practices in Edinburgh. He has had some success using minute trepanations to alleviate swelling. It may be that your father's injury created an accumulation of blood, and if so, this procedure might relieve it."

I took the note from him, still dabbing at my eyes. "Thank you," I managed.

"My pleasure. And of course, should your father experience any change in his condition, come to me at once. I see charity cases two nights each week, at the poor house and the brothel. Otherwise, I am usually here." He rose and shook each of our hands. "You have a fine mind in there, sir. I hate to see it imprisoned by something as mundane as words."

We left the office and began walking back to the house, but my father suddenly stopped me in the street and hugged me. "Not your fault," he said in my ear.

"I should have thought to try," I said. "All those weeks,

when you were struggling just to make *sounds*—"

"Hands shook more." He drew back and smiled at me. "Brave girl," he said. "*Mine*."

I smiled back, though cold tears stung my cheeks. He wiped them away and then angled his head. "Walk?"

"Do you feel strong enough?" I looked doubtfully at his hip. "The road is quite steep."

"Beer," he said slyly.

"Incorrigible," I chided, but I took his arm again and we walked down to the bay.

This time we walked down the main road rather than cutting through the maze of alleys surrounding our cottage. I made note of the shops we passed, while my father touched his hat at every woman, young and old, sometimes twisting us both about in his efforts. Horses strained to pull carts loaded with coal and fish, while children ran in their wake to gather stray pieces. The smells were pungent in the cold winter air; I could hardly imagine what a stench it would be in summer.

There were no birds, no redwings or robins as at home, no gulls or gannets circling overhead; but there would be no birds in Medby as long as the beast was nearby.

The road curved slightly and then we saw the bay, a slate-colored expanse dappled with foam, and the crowding ships that filled the walled harbor. Further out was the ship we suspected was the *Leviathan*, fatter and taller than the others.

"Bloody frigate," my father blurted out.

"We think that is Thomas Masterson's ship," I said in a

lower voice. "The one he's calling *Leviathan*."

My father tried to speak again but it came out as an incoherent sound. "Take your time," I said.

"Picking fights," he finally managed.

"Picking fights," I agreed.

With this grim statement we reached the waterfront, wending our way between the throngs of sailors, sellers, and some dubiously-dressed women towards the water's edge. It was truly a magnificent bay, far grander than our little one at home, with a wide expanse of flat beach where the surf rolled and crashed dramatically. To our left, the harbor wall sheltered piers and shipbuilders; far to the right, we could see stairs had been built down from the cliffs, and there were wheeled huts lined up neatly on the beach.

"Sea bathing," a passing sailor said as he walked past. "Too cold for it now, miss," he added with a wink. "But I'll warm you if you like."

"Prat," my father replied haughtily.

"Just a joke, granddad," he called over his shoulder.

"I should use him to practice Mister Windham's techniques," I muttered. My face was warm, and I was distinctly aware of other sailors looking my way.

"Just words," my father said, but he started us walking again, heading towards the harbor wall. "Better married," he added.

My thoughts flew to Jo, how she had held me last night—I kept my gaze on the bright bay and the looming form of the *Leviathan*. Now I could see she was flying England's colors and coiled on her prow was a carved figure of a serpent. Not a precise depiction of the creature, but there was something about its head, and especially its yellow eyes, that suggested its creator knew of the ship's namesake.

"Only one," my father said.

"But he will not be without help," I whispered. "I just cannot understand why. Surely he would profit more from rising tensions than a decisive act of war?"

My father had slowed. His brow was furrowed, an expression I remembered from his debates with Uncle Stuart. How long ago that seemed now.

"Different profit?" He looked at me thoughtfully.

"What else can you profit from, besides money? Land? Goods?"

"Power," my father said.

The word chilled me. *Lord Masterson*, Mrs. Lambert had said. I looked at the boat, then at my father, who sketched points above his head, describing a crown. "He wouldn't dare," I said. "Surely, recent events would have shown …" I trailed off, watching the sparkling, opaque sea. "Though, the Pretender did not have a monster at his command," I whispered.

My father tugged on my arm. "Tell Smith," he said.

I shook my head. "This is all speculation, still. We need to find this Captain Herbert and give Jo a chance."

Lost in our thoughts, we continued around the bay. My face was starting to ache from the cold and I knew my father would be chilled, yet I could not stop looking. Dinghies full of eager, laughing men were drawing onto the beach, where they climbed over each other in their haste to get on land

and crowd into the many public houses lining the streets. My father coughed and switched sides, as if to shield me from the sight—and what would he think, what might he say, if I confessed that I longed to be one of those men?

But then I saw the building, and forgot my troubled thoughts. I stopped us and nodded across the street. "Thomas Masterson's company," I said in a low voice.

A small crowd of men had gathered around the doorway which I could now see clearly. In bright gold lettering was written,

Thos. Masterson & Co.

And underneath, in smaller black script,

Fine Imports & Exports

The crowd seemed to be waiting expectantly, muttering among themselves. A few traded a bottle back and forth. As they dawdled, a carriage drew up, a brouette drawn by a burly man with a scarf over his face. Out of it came an elegant—no, a *stunning* woman. Her fur-trimmed mantle did little to hide the crimson satin of her skirts, or her slim waistline perched atop her broad hoops. Her profile was exquisite, a flash of a powdered and rouged face with pursed red lips above a decisive jawline. Her rich cascade of black hair was topped with a feather and lace-swathed hat that seemed to float. The men parted like the sea, letting her walk grandly inside, turning sideways to fit her hoops through the door; then they closed again behind her. Only when she had vanished did the brouette depart.

It was an astonishing display, like watching a court lady enter a stable. I glanced at my father and saw he was equally surprised.

"A question for Jo," I said.

The crowd kept growing, men drifting towards us as if summoned. My father trembled with agitation, his face pale beneath his chapped cheeks. "Not good," he muttered.

Looking around, I saw a deep-set doorway and steered him to it. Here, we could still see much of the crowd, yet we were spared the cutting winds from the bay. He leaned heavily against the door and I caught his gaze. "We can go home, if you're not feeling well—"

"Fine," he said hoarsely, then smiled at me. "Beer, yes?"

"Yes, yes," I sighed, craning my head down the street again.

The door of the building opened, yet no one emerged. Still, the crowd quieted, a congregation ready for a sermon. I wondered if Jo had her greatcoat to hand; the door would create a draft …

"What are they waiting for?" I wondered aloud.

"Crew list," a man's voice said.

We whirled about to see a man leaning against the wall behind us. He touched his hat. "It's the final list for the *Leviathan*," he explained. "Word was that it would be announced today."

"The *Leviathan*?" I kept my tone light. "An unusual name for a ship."

He pointed at the bay. "She's the frigate, just past the others."

"And they're so eager to sail on her?"

"Word is they had three times as many offers as they needed."

"Three times? They need work so badly?" A hush had fallen over the crowd as a tall, dark-skinned man stepped forward in a fresh suit that was as fine as the one he wore last night. Mr. Morrow.

"Not for work," the man murmured, leaning even closer. "They are eager to spill French blood, and perhaps English as well."

From behind Mr. Morrow emerged a well-dressed man so like Edward Masterson, both my father and I gasped. This Masterson was younger, with his own pale hair drawn back in a neat queue—but the resemblance was unmistakable, down to the haughty air with which he surveyed the crowd.

"Masterson!" the men cheered. "Masterson! Masterson!"

I could not breathe for my sudden panic. I felt imprisoned by the stranger on one side of me and my father on the other, yet I dared not turn away. The crowd kept roaring his name like one vast, baying animal. It seemed as if it would never end. Then Thomas Masterson raised one slim hand and the noise silenced as if smothered. Slowly, gracefully, he drew a small book from inside his coat and thumbed through its pages while the men watched him with the mute adoration of children.

"O Lord, how manifold are thy works," he read aloud, the syllables beautifully enunciated. "In wisdom hast thou made them all: the earth is full of thy riches. So is this great and wide sea, wherein are things creeping innumerable, both small and great beasts. There go the ships: there is that leviathan, whom thou hast made to play therein. These wait all upon thee; that thou mayest give them their *meat* in due season."

It was last spring yet again, his rhythmic cadences a perfect replica of his brother's. Even I felt drawn in, and my father's expression was becoming dazed as it had all those months ago—

—and then his voice stopped, and everyone shook themselves as if suddenly awakened from a dream.

Mr. Morrow cleared his throat and with a flourish, snapped open a folded paper. "The following," he declared, "are invited to crew the *Leviathan* in her maiden voyage, and may God's will be done."

A cheer went up at this and at every name he then recited, on and on until it built into another roar. My father pressed close to me.

"Two ships lost this year, when there were none for some time," the man said, his breath warm against my ear. "It's a wonder they haven't rioted, when our King does nothing to protect them and Mister Masterson so persuasive."

The crowd was dispersing, and thankfully the man took a step back. My breath returned, and my wits as well. "You have made a study of Mister Masterson?"

He seemed not to hear me. Instead, he stared thoughtfully at the bay. I took the opportunity to study his profile. No schoolboy, but not yet greying; fine clothes, but dirty and worn; a chin held high, but a wig that was some years out of date.

Then he turned back to me and the sly smile on his face made him oddly handsome. "I am indeed studying him, as are you, Miss Daniels."

My stomach vanished. My hand dropped to my pocket, where the little knife still nestled from the previous night. "How do you know my name, sir?"

The man looked around again, but I did not once take my eyes from him, as Mr. Windham had instructed. "Perhaps we should go somewhere else," he said.

"I would have your answer now, *sir*," I said. My voice did not waver. Behind me, my father was pulling at my arm—trying, I think, to step between us.

The man moved close to me. "Because we have a mutual friend named Smith," he said in a low voice. "I am Captain Herbert. I am your contact here, and your father looks remarkably thirsty. There is a quiet inn just up the street; we can speak freely there." He smiled again, that too-bright smile. "The first round is on me."

CHAPTER VIII

Captain Herbert

The inn was as Captain Herbert described, but I knew that was no proof of his trustworthiness. He had shown us his papers, but those could be faked; he claimed to know Smith, but that could have been a ruse. Beyond that, the Captain seemed disinterested in *my* proofs, or, indeed, my trustworthiness on any matter. He was far too busy sharing his opinions.

"You will have to watch out for Morrow," he was explaining, tapping the table with his forefinger like a schoolmaster wanting attention. My father, bless him, leaned in a little more with each tap, until I feared for his cravat, which dangled perilously near his ale. "He is loyal to Masterson—or owned by him, which amounts to the same thing."

"Owned?" I blurted the word out, which earned me a stern look from the Captain. "You think him a slave?"

"Or as like. It's their natural inclination after all." The Captain gave me another look, as if wondering who was this fool that Mr. Smith had sent. "Now, where was I? The *Leviathan* is set to sail this very weekend. It gives us little time to intervene beforehand. If she finds anything, *anything* that we can use against Masterson, Miss Chase—"

"Mister Read," I corrected.

"—Read," he said, irritated now. "She must come straight to me."

"*He* must come to me," I corrected him again. At the Captain's darkening expression I smiled pleasantly. "Mister Smith advised us to maintain our identities consistently, the better to be taken for man and wife."

As I spoke, I saw it, though it vanished swiftly: a far uglier expression on the Captain's face. Not anger but … a kind of interest, one that made me feel decidedly uncomfortable. "How clever of him," he said.

"What happens if Mister Read finds something?" I asked.

"Then I get word to Smith. He has men in Grimsby who can be here within a day. We have already alerted the magistrate that Masterson is of interest to His Majesty. The local authorities are not pleased with his rabble-rousing nor his new ship. They are as eager to be rid of him as we are."

"And if we do not find anything, and he sails?"

The Captain looked around, then leaned in further. "Then the Navy will ensure he never engages another ship. But then we will have a martyr on our hands, Miss Daniels, and that will create more problems. Plus, there is the matter of these rumors about sea monsters. Anyone would think we were a country of savages," he added with disgust.

"Missus Read," I corrected. "Is it savage to believe the evidence of your eyes?"

The Captain blinked, then smiled. "Ah, yes. Mister Smith mentioned something about this—an encounter with a most terrifying snake, as I recall?"

"A snake that did more damage than a cannon, Captain," I replied. "Where can we find you?"

He drew out a card and wrote an address on the back. "It's just off the market road," he explained. "I have leased the property, so you can come and go without notice. I hope to hear from you soon, Miss Daniels."

"Missus Read," I corrected again, my exasperation nearly getting the better of me. "And now we must take our leave, Captain Herbert. My father needs to rest. He tires easily and he still must make it home."

"I can send for a chair—"

"That would look a fine thing: a clerk's father-in-law, coming home in a sedan chair." I smiled, pleased that I had disconcerted him. "Oh, and Captain? There was a woman who came to Mister Masterson's office this morning. What do you know of her?"

He rose and helped me from my chair. "That, Missus Read, is Madame Viart. French, owner of Medby's only proper brothel, and, it seems, Thomas Masterson's mistress. Though, to be clear, a French mistress is not a crime." He smirked at the latter.

"Indeed." I thought again of that perfect, pretty face and the richness of her clothing, and my stomach clenched.

"He goes every Friday and spends the night, entertaining the local nobility at his own expense—and himself, of course." The Captain went to the window and peered outside. "I would see you home, but I suspect it would be better if we left separately—?" At my assent, he kissed my hand and shook my father's. "A pleasure to meet you both."

Outside, my father said, "Informative fellow."

"If he is who he claims to be," I replied. Surreptitiously, I wiped my hand on my cloak, but I could not undo the sensation of having been touched by something unpleasant.

When I finished my recounting over supper, Jo shook her head. "I wish I had been there," she said. "He doesn't sound like Smith's usual sort." At my downcast expression, she touched my hand under the table. "Well. Let us say he is indeed our intermediary. Unfortunately, I have little chance of getting anything useful before the *Leviathan* sails. I was nearly turned away this morning, and when they finally deigned to give me work, it was tallying orders of ship's biscuit, of all things—and my prospects are not much better." She ticked off her fingers. "No one works on the entirety of Masterson's holdings: every account is its own ledger, and each clerk is assigned to only a few accounts. The ledgers reside in a locked cabinet in Masterson's office, to which he has the sole key. There's also a large wallet full of papers, a wallet with what looked like *that* shape embossed on its front, but I barely glimpsed it—I cannot be certain."

"Symbol or no, those papers might be useful," I said.

"I'm certain they would be, but we have to get that key to find out." She smiled grimly. "Unfortunately no one seems like a possible ally. They either adore him or are terrified of losing their positions—or both. The general belief is that he's a great man who will change the future of England."

I thought of last night's plaintive wail, and today's roaring crowd. "What is our next step?"

"Well, I'll keep looking for a start, even the smallest evidence of wrongdoing—"

"Pardon me," Mr. Simmons said from the kitchen, "but isn't buying a frigate and inciting treason enough?"

Jo twisted around in her chair. "For God's sake, Mister Simmons, come sit. We don't have to shout like we're in an alehouse."

I looked at my father, visibly startled, then at Mr. Simmons, who hesitated in the doorway.

"Isn't there another chair?" Jo half-rose, looking around. "Take mine, then, I've finished eating—"

"I'll fetch one," I said quickly, going to the front room before anyone could speak further. There I found a chair and carried it to the table. It was small, but I thought if Jo yielded her place to Mr. Simmons my father might react poorly. As it was he seemed bewildered, a surprise that only increased when he found himself face-to-face with Mr. Simmons, who sat down gingerly, as if chair and table alike might shatter at his touch.

"You were saying?" Jo prompted.

"Only, ah—" He swallowed, his eyes everywhere but on my father's face. "Only that I thought inciting treason was against the law."

"Very true, but Thomas Masterson has two things in his favor: money, and well-placed friends," Jo explained. "We knew before we came that he might have a minister aiding him. Today, I saw correspondence from several notable gentlemen in banking, trade, even munitions. Besides, the broadsides speak only against the French, not the King—he has chosen his words with some care."

"If we cannot find evidence," I said, "perhaps we should focus on stopping the beast, and let the Navy deal with Mister Masterson?" At her thoughtful look, I gestured in the direction of the bay. "We know it's nearby. If we could lure it away, he would be nothing more than a wealthy madman."

"Are you suggesting we murder a woman?" Jo asked.

My poor father made a choking noise and Mr. Simmons hurried behind him to pound on his back, giving me a disapproving look as he did so. "Perhaps we should speak of something else," he said.

"You cannot tell me that it only eats Englishwomen," I said. "It's an animal! Surely we can tempt it with something else—fish, cattle? A horse, perhaps?"

"So, you want to kill a horse," Jo said, grinning as my father squeaked again.

"Butchery," he managed to get out, gasping. "For God's …"

"We're in a seaside village and the countryside is filled with sheep," I said, patting my father's hand and giving Jo a stern look. "I'm sure someone would be more than happy to give us their offal."

Jo was still grinning. I kicked her shin under the table and she yelped, then stuck her tongue out at me, which set me to giggling in turn.

"It's not the worst idea," Mr. Simmons said as he resumed his seat. "Especially if your father and I help you plan this."

"Yes, God," my father said, still heaving. "Not alone."

It wasn't quite what I had wanted—I had fancied myself investigating alone, *doing* something, while Jo toiled away under Mr. Masterson's nose. But it was something, and we were running out of time.

That night I climbed into bed but Jo hesitated, fussing over her clothes and frowning at everything and nothing. When she lay beside me she was stiff, staring at the ceiling; but when I started to turn away, her arm slipped around me and she buried her face in my neck.

"Your father seems to like him," she mumbled against my skin.

"Who?" I asked, though I suspected I knew.

"Captain Herbert." She uttered the name with distaste.

I smiled into her hair. "My father likes any man under sixty as a marriage prospect." I wiggled lower, trying to catch her eye. "That doesn't mean I do."

Still, her gloomy expression lingered. "He's a captain and not put off by your spying. Not a common cut of man."

"Oh, I wouldn't say he was pleased with my work." I shrugged when she squinted at me. "He seemed to think me either a fool or something, well …"

"Go on," Jo said in a low voice.

"Something titillating," I admitted. "Two women playing at man and wife. He made me feel wrong," I added, surprised at my own anger. "If that is an uncommon man, I don't want anything to do with such."

"Perhaps I shall challenge him to a duel, to show how well we play our roles?" I pinched her hip and her mouth curved against my neck. "It's a slight to your honor, and as your husband—"

"You will do no such thing!" I pinched her again, only to be tickled in turn. "Be serious, Jo."

"I am being serious," she said, kissing my neck. "We're risking ourselves and he wants to peep through the keyhole! I doubt he's our man, and we have no time for games."

"Such as we're playing now?" I asked breathlessly, for her hands were everywhere, tickling and poking—

And then something else, far more pleasurable.

"This is no game, Caroline," she whispered against my neck.

"Wait … what you just did …" I could not find words for what I wanted. I could only demonstrate, fumbling like a child; but she divined my intent with some deeper instinct of her own. Her eyes glowing as she leaned over and blew out the lamp before divesting us both of our shifts.

CHAPTER IX

The Cove

I saw Jo off the next morning, only to hear my father calling. He was in his room, upright and dressed in his banyan. He waved a note at me written in his new, spindly handwriting:

Mr. Simmons has gone for information.

At once, panicked questions sprang to mind—what information? Who was he talking to, would he be careful?—but I realized my poor father looked famished. I helped him downstairs and settled him in the kitchen. There, I found our breakfast laid out and the chocolate already warm.

As we sat down to eat, Mr. Simmons returned, grinning boyishly. He hurried to the kitchen and when he returned, he was once more our Mr. Simmons, sober and ready to serve more rolls, though the corner of his mouth kept twitching.

"Oh, for goodness' sake," I exclaimed. "Fetch yourself a plate and tell us what you learned."

He hesitated, but only for a moment. When he returned with his plate, he sat down in a dignified manner and spread his napkin. Only then did he say, "I think I have found the beast."

My father exclaimed, "Well done!" while at the same time I said, "Not in the bay?"

He smiled at his plate. I realized he was preening from his success. "Not in *this* bay," he said.

Already, I was thinking of clothes, a packed lunch, how far I might have to walk—or would I do better to hire a horse? "North or south?"

"North," he said. "As it happens, we're right at the start of a headland." He sketched a line on the tabletop. "The coast turns just north of us and forms a cove. It's small and deep, you can't see it from the road. There were not one but two accidents just this summer, folks falling and breaking their necks on the rocks. Now, everyone avoids it—a great help if you're trying to hide something."

My father snorted at the latter, but I was already rising. Mr. Simmons gave me a keen look. "The accidents were plausible, Miss. It's very difficult to get down to the cove: the steps are treacherous and the landlord said you could yell for days without being heard. I don't think you should go alone."

I looked at my father. "But if the way is difficult—"

"I can set your father aright for a few hours," he said. "You and I can ride over the headland. I have already seen to two horses. We'll bring the spyglass and return before dinner."

It was an eminently sensible plan, yet it made my hackles rise. It was to be *my* task, as Jo's equal, and Mr. Simmons and my father merely our credibility—

But only a fool would react so to a sound plan given by a trusted friend. I assented, set about helping to clear the breakfast things, then changed for what promised to be an invigorating ride.

It was thankfully overcast when we set out. In our brief time in Medby, I had already learned to love lowering clouds, for they took the bite out of the cold. Our horses were good, sturdy animals, seemingly used to the winding, uphill streets. As we surmounted the headland, the narrow cottages gave way to scrubby trees and windswept pastures. Here, too, was a church, the first we had seen, its tower pitted by what Mr. Simmons declared to be cannon fire. That, plus a ruined fort at the furthest edge of the headland, spoke of past wars and sounded an ominous note for our excursion.

On the far side of the headland, we paused to survey our surroundings. Behind us, the houses stood snug against the cold, their chimneys steadily smoking; before us was the northern horizon, a grey sea dotted with a few boats. Here, the wind was far more gusting, with no sign of livestock in the fields. I saw a crude hut, but no other sign of human habitation.

Then we descended through a copse of splintering brush and stunted trees, and saw what we were searching for.

The cove was, indeed, hidden. In places the cliffs seemed to overhang the water, hiding how deep the inlet was. At its entrance, the surf churned violently, sending up magnificent sprays, but inside the water was much calmer. Though my memories of our spring encounter were fragmented, I thought it just large enough to shelter the beast. With a glance around, Mr. Simmons handed me the spyglass and I surveyed the cove thoroughly. It seemed as if steps had been chiseled into the rock, but if so, the path wound somewhere beneath us.

"Can we get closer?" I asked, dismounting my horse.

Mr. Simmons tied the animals to a stunted tree and took my arm. In the guise of a strolling couple, we made our way to the edge where he gestured grandly, as if describing the vista to me.

"What are you looking for, Miss?" he asked.

"Evidence of the beast, and its keepers." I craned my head around and his arm went rigid as he steadied me. "Are those the steps leading down?"

"Wait." He stepped between myself and the cliff edge, ground in his heel, and carefully leaned over. "Yes, but they're worn to almost nothing. I can see how a fellow might break his neck on them."

"Where do they come out?"

He nodded further along the edge and we made our way towards the spot. The wind suddenly gusted, catching at my skirts, and I was knocked backwards as if I were no more than a leaf. Mr. Simmons tightened his grip. "Same thing happened to Missus once," he said. "Went for a walk by the water when we were courting; wind nearly took her out to sea. I always walk on the outside now."

At the mention of Mrs. Simmons, my face grew warm. Here I was annoyed by his planning, while he had left behind his wife to help us … and then I remembered his expression when Jo kissed me goodbye. "Mister Simmons," I began slowly, "I have neglected to say … that is, if you feel as she does …"

"Jane always wanted a daughter," he said. "Babies never made her broody, but a little girl to dress up … Well. God decided for us, so she became a mother in other ways. You, Emily … may she forgive me, but I think if Emily had lived, Jane would have had an easier time with Miss Chase. Two in one year and all."

I took a breath before I spoke. "I'm not dead, Mister Simmons."

"And I'm not saying it right." He stopped then, sucking on his teeth as he thought. I had a sudden recollection of being a little girl and asking to ride a horse for the first time: that same pained consideration. "I've known women like your Miss Chase. Jane never believed me, but there's always a few in the army. Not the ones who wanted to be near their men—they got weeded out quick. But there were always a few who came in with men's names, acted like us, dressed like us, and were as good as any of the lads." He grinned. "When you're facing the French, or mad-as-hell Scots, you don't give a damn if the one firing next to you is a man or a woman or a horse in a uniform. Just as long as they keep shooting."

I gaped at him. "There were women soldiers?"

"Yes, Miss."

"And your fellows … they did not … mind?"

"Oh, a few minded and a few tried to be clever. Why go to town to get a leg over when it's right in the next tent?" He flushed. "Begging your pardon, Miss."

"I know what a leg over means, Mister Simmons." I shook my head in wonderment. "I just cannot believe these women were allowed to pursue such a career unmolested."

His expression grew somber. "Maybe they were, though I never heard of it. We sorted out those who thought to try. I always wondered, too, if there were more … with one of them, it was more than a year before we knew what she really was, and by then she was just good ol' Till. Couldn't think of her as anything else." He shrugged again. "All of which is to say, Miss, that I see your Miss Chase a little different than Jane does, and I know my Jane. She'll come around. Wrote her the other day and told her just how happy you are, even with all this worry." He gestured vaguely. "She'd rather have you happy than anything else, even if it's not how she pictured it."

There were so many things I wanted to say, but they were lost in a rush of homesickness. When again I could speak, I simply said, "When next you write her? Please tell her I miss her."

In response, Mr. Simmons nodded and began leading me down the steps.

I thought at first he was being overprotective, keeping me pressed behind him, but the thought vanished as we descended. The wind was fierce, whistling along the cliff face, and my skirts twisted so violently, I feared I would pull us both down. Why had I not donned one of Jo's costumes? It would be quite a denouement for me to come so far, only to die from my dress.

At last, though, we seemed to descend beneath the winds which now roared overhead. Indeed, the cove was another world: beyond some invisible barrier, the elements whipped about, but here there was only a breeze. Below us, the water lapped at all sides, and from our closer vantage I saw a cave of sorts cut at the base of the cliffs, with a sandy floor that appeared and disappeared beneath the water.

Sloshing inside, never quite leaving, was a mass of beige fabric. Mr. Simmons halted so abruptly I nearly fell atop him. "Perhaps I should go on alone," he said.

"I have seen worse, Mister Simmons," I replied. For it was true.

He seemed about to protest, but instead we continued on, slower now as the steps became increasingly slippery. At last, we reached a kind of platform from which one could leap to the cave floor. But we could see all we needed.

In the cave there were *pieces*. There was no other word for them. They were scattered about like a butcher's scraps, rotted to the point of putrescence. Clothing too: pieces of slimy linen, cloth ties twisting in the water like snakes. But what arrested my gaze were the pieces where there were still patches of skin, large and small, dark brown to a greying white. Unlike his brother, it seemed that Mr. Masterson favored a much broader diet for the beast, throwing men and women of every race into its maw. Who were these poor souls, treated like slop, as Mr. Smith had described?

Mr. Simmons made a gagging noise and drew back, but I inched forward on the platform, for there was something else inside, something familiar—

Painted on the back of the cave in something moist and swarming with flies was a circle of jagged triangles radiating undulating limbs.

The face of the beast, of the true Leviathan.

I shifted my grip on the rocky wall and my feet slid out

from under me, causing me to topple forward with a cry. The sharp rocks raked my arm as Mr. Simmons caught me around the waist and slung me back onto the platform beside him.

But not before my arms had plunged into the water.

I held up my dripping arm. The sleeves were in tatters and blood ran freely from a deep cut the length of my forearm. Mr. Simmons exclaimed something about caution and pressed his handkerchief over the cut, but I felt momentarily disembodied. Had not this very thing happened last spring, when my father and I went walking with Edward Masterson? I had cut my hand, he had taken the handkerchief and blotted my blood—

—and then thrown it into the sea.

I looked out the mouth of the cove. Beyond the churn the sea was a steady palette of grey ripples. Mr. Simmons bound my arm, but I could only stare with fatalistic anticipation.

Far out to sea, a shimmering black curve broke the water, then disappeared again.

"Miss?" Mr. Simmons shook me. "Miss, are you all right? You lost a fair bit of blood."

"We must go," I whispered.

Again the black curve broke the water, sliding forward smoothly amidst the crashing surf. Closer than before.

I looked at Mr. Simmons then. "It's coming," I said more loudly. "We must *go*."

We hurried up the steps, going as fast as we dared on the slick stone. My arm throbbed. Beneath us, the black curve rose again, just before the mouth of the cove, and I heard Mr. Simmons gasp. When we reached the wind we hugged the cliff face and inched upwards. The air pressed tears from my eyes, my skirts whipped and twisted, and silently I apologized to Jo and my father and Missus Simmons all, for being so, so stupid—

"Mother of God," Mr. Simmons suddenly cried, halting above me. I followed his downward gaze and my stomach vanished.

The Leviathan was nestled in the cove as neatly as a bird in its nest. Beneath the surface of the water was a coiled black shadow that seemed to fill the space from cliff wall to cliff wall. It rolled with the surf, shifting and twisting. Long, fat tentacles slid into the cave where they writhed and rippled, shuffling through the debris.

The wind was slapping us. I pushed at Mr. Simmons. "Keep going," I gasped.

We started climbing once more, trying to ignore the wet, slapping sounds beneath us as the beast moved about its lair. At last, the cliff top came into view. Mr. Simmons reached the grass and hauled me up beside him. Then, as if of one mind, we both crawled to the edge and peered back into the cove.

The beast had stuffed its entire head into the cave, wiggling obscenely in its search. Loud sucking sounds marked every change in its position. I knew, however, that the fresh meat it sought was not there, and had not been for some time.

It drew back, snapping its head free and up towards the sky, and the ring of teeth opened and emitted a high-pitched wail that made us clap our hands to our ears. It was the same sound from that first night, a sound like nothing else on earth, and I knew I would hear that wail in my dreams, perhaps for the rest of my life.

It landed back in the water with a crash that sent up spray past the tops of the cliffs, spattering us and the grass alike. We both flinched and scurried back from the edge, readying for an attack—

—but nothing came. After a few minutes, we went to the edge once more.

The cove was empty.

Mr. Simmons was breathing hard. He looked at me with a ghastly expression. "That is what you saw last spring," he said, his voice shaking. "What killed poor Emily."

I nodded. I was breathless myself, my heart racing.

"And still, you came here?"

Again I nodded, breathing deeply until I found my voice once more. "We must get word," I finally said. "Word to Mister Smith."

"That the beast is here?"

"That the beast is here," I agreed, "and I think—I think he's starving it." At Mr. Simmons' perplexed look I explained, "Those remains looked old, old and rotten—and how quickly it came? I have heard nothing about any missing persons, have you?"

"Nothing save those accidents last summer," Mr. Simmons admitted, looking at the sea with alarm. "But why keep it hungry? Surely that would make the beast harder to control?"

I could only shake my head. Harder to control, but quicker to attack, more violent? I could not say with certainty, and, in a sense, it did not matter. What mattered is that we had but a few days left, if that, and then many people would die.

CHAPTER X

Plots

I had expected Jo to be impressed by our discovery, but in that I was disappointed. She listened to Mr. Simmons and I as we recounted our adventure with a face devoid of expression. Once we had finished, she simply nodded and set to cutting up her meat. I was about to speak again when she said in a bland voice, "Well. There's nothing for it now but to get Masterson's keys. He is hiding something in those cabinets. With luck, it will be something we can swiftly arrest him for."

"Force it?" my father offered.

"I would rather not put his guard up," Jo said. "We want him arrested, not on the run." She looked at me. "And I think I know a way to get them."

I met her gaze, still bristling from her disinterest. "Go on," I said.

"Madame Viart. If he stays true to form, he will be going to the brothel tomorrow for his various entertainments ..." She trailed off significantly.

Mr. Simmons coughed and my father turned bright red. I just looked at Jo, trying to check my sudden nausea.

"It's a large ring, full of keys of all sizes," she continued. "If we can get to it while he's about his business, it will be some time before he notices one small key missing."

"You are going to a brothel." I felt sick, sick inside and out.

"They also host card games and apparently their brandy is the best in Medby. I'm sure half the men in town will be there."

"They don't admit just anyone," Mr. Simmons put in. When we all looked at him, he had the grace to look abashed. "I've heard it costs a pretty penny and if you try anything, there are a few handy lads who will do for you."

"Which is why we'll need that captain of yours," Jo said.

"Oh, he's my captain now?" I could not see, for everything was swimming. The food on my plate was suddenly a tasteless mess.

"A healthy man of rank, idling away in Medby? Unless he's a saint, he's been there—and he can get me in." She took a breath. "Or us, if you prefer," she added tonelessly. "My blue suit fits you well enough."

At that my father made a choking noise. Mr. Simmons hurried to him and patted his back, giving Jo and I a disapproving look.

"What is so upsetting?" Jo asked.

"It's a *brothel*," I said.

"A bloody brothel!" my father burst out at the same time. He covered his face with his napkin, coughing into it.

"They are women no different than ourselves, doing what men and women have always done," Jo said.

"That's not the point," I snapped.

"Then what is the point?" An edge was creeping into her

voice. "We need to ascertain his purpose. That ship sails this weekend and *apparently* the beast is starving. We know the key will be available tomorrow night as it will not be at any other time. Besides, there will be so many going in and out we won't even be noticed."

"You mean *you* won't be noticed," I retorted.

"I said you could come with me if you're so worried." Her voice rose. "And it should be less dangerous than climbing around that bloody cove!"

There was an anger in her voice I had never heard before, one laced with hurt. I felt wounded in turn. I dashed from the room, blinded by sudden tears, nearly falling up the stairs in my haste and throwing myself on the bed—*our* bed. I had hurt her and she was hurting me, but we were partners. Was I to stay home while she risked herself? All that tangled in my mind with the memory of Madame Viart's pristine beauty, now flanked by a dozen women as beautiful as herself, women without the burden of family, women who never fumbled or made mistakes, women like paintings beckoning naked from the softest silken featherbeds …

There was a creak on the stairs and then a soft knock. "Caroline," Jo whispered. "Can I come in?"

I could not answer. She opened the door cautiously, took one look at me, and swiftly crossed the room. Her arms around me only made me weep harder. I wanted to protest, but instead I found myself sobbing into her neck.

"I'm sorry for speaking so. I …" She took a breath. "You frightened me," she said more calmly, "and I … I was hurt that you went with Mister Simmons and not me."

I was quieting in her arms, my tears tapering off to shuddering gasps. "We are partners," I forced out. "In risk, in everything."

She was silent.

"Or am I supposed to sit around like a, like a *wife*, keeping house and, and *knitting* while you risk yourself?" I pulled away. "If so, then I will get the next coach home and to hell with you, Joanna Chase, to hell with you and all your plots!"

Her eyes were full and red, but at my speech she made a noise that I realized was swallowed laughter, a laughter that bubbled forth when I pulled further away. "Heaven forbid," she gasped, wiping roughly at her eyes. "Heaven forbid I drive you to *knit*, darling." When I only scowled she took my hand in hers. "If you truly think the brothel a bad idea we'll come up with something else. All right?"

I kept scowling, but I felt myself soften inside. "No, you're right. It is the best opportunity we'll have in this short time."

"But you're upset, still. Or frightened ...?" She wiggled closer to me. "The only risk, to my mind, is that you'll see some adorable French chit and I will have to woo you away, which will confuse everyone in the damn place—oh no, no, what did I say?"

My eyes were welling again. "It's only ... she is so much more *woman* than I am, and she ... that you might ..." I could not go on.

"Who?" She screwed up her nose as she thought, then laughed again, low and soft. "Oh, Madame Viart! Oh yes, she is much more woman than anyone alive." She drew me close. "A vain French princess who cares only for herself?

Good God, Caroline, I think I'd rather face the Leviathan. Far less painful."

"Jo," I began.

"I was going to suggest you play cards with Captain Herbert while I sneak in by other means, but now *I'm* worried," she said with a frown. "You are far more adorable than I, and the French do love costumes."

I gaped at her. "I am not going to play cards in a brothel! My father would die!"

"Must he know of it?" When I glared at her, she laughed. "Well, we are both going, Missus Read, that much is certain. One of us can plausibly get through the front door with this captain to vouch for us. The other will have to be more clever." At my silence, she shrugged. "Or we can simply wait until the beast attacks, and hope we have enough witnesses to the carnage to hang Masterson and avoid a war."

I was sulking. I knew what a picture I made, but a part of my mind was following a different set of thoughts. Thinking of my father had made me think of Dr. Denham, and reminded me of a remark he had made.

"Perhaps there is a way," I admitted.

Friday dawned clear and cold. The house was unusually somber as we went about our morning routines. My gaze kept drifting to the table where three rings of old keys lay. Jo and I had stayed up late practicing their stealthy removal from pockets and tabletops, hooks and bedposts; how swiftly we could prise the rings open, remove one, and return it.

At dinnertime, Jo came home and we set out to see Captain Herbert. Walking arm-in-arm down the road from our cottage, the dim afternoon sunlight catching the rooftops, I felt unusually … visible. In my village, Jo was a familiar face now. On the journey to Medby, we had passed through places so quickly I had not given a thought to those around us. But now, we were strolling in broad daylight as husband and wife. It was wonderful and frightening all at once. Part of me wanted to sing with joy and part of me was knotted with dread at every curious glance, every brush of a body against us. When a boy suddenly reached up, I thought he was going to pull Jo's hat and wig off, but he merely slapped a hanging sign. When a man strode towards us with raised fists, I braced for violence, but he pushed past us and began yelling at someone else.

Jo glanced at me. "People see what they want to see," she murmured. "No one will twig unless they want to, and no one has a reason to want to."

I smiled tightly as we passed a knot of women, all talking in low voices and eyeing us. "I am more afraid for you," I whispered. "Doesn't it frighten you, what might happen if you're discovered?"

She pursed her lips, thinking, as we turned towards the market road. "Well. Let's say, when I was younger I enjoyed the thrill, and then I simply got used to it. Now, though?" She looked at me again, a sad smile tugging at her lips. "I will confess to being a little rattled, though from the best possible cause."

It took me a moment to understand, and then I could

only blush, pulling my hood lower to hide my embarrassment. She squeezed my arm but said nothing further. We continued in silence until at last we reached Captain Herbert's door.

It took vigorous knocking to elicit footsteps and a muttered curse, and when he flung open the door in only his shirt and breeches, it was plain that we had woken him. "What did you do?" he demanded.

I bristled at this and Jo gave my arm another squeeze. "We have need of you, Captain Herbert," she said. "May we enter, or shall we discuss our business in full view of Medby?"

He blinked at Jo. "Ah, the mister," he said, stepping aside and letting us enter. "I see why you got the breeches role. First door on the right, ladies."

Jo gave him a slit-eyed look, then turned so only I could see her face. *Your captain*, she mouthed at me, smirking when I made an exasperated noise.

We found ourselves in a parlor as disheveled as its lodger. Someone had decorated the room in simple, pleasant furnishings; now, however, it looked as if an animal had taken up residence. There were clothes everywhere, dirty dishes everywhere, bottles everywhere. A heady smell of tobacco smoke and sweat flavored the stuffy air. A table held evidence of a card game, but Captain Herbert swept this onto the floor, drew out two chairs, and sprawled in a third.

Before I sat, Jo touched my arm and then she drew out her handkerchief, making a show of wiping off both seats for us. She remained standing until I was seated; only then did she sweep aside her coattails and lower herself gingerly onto the chair. "You must be quite the friend of Smith's," she remarked.

"I am," the captain said shortly. He tapped out a pipe on the table, then began to pack in fresh tobacco. "Well? What do you need from me?"

"We need you to take me to play cards at Madame Viart's brothel," Jo said.

Whatever Captain Herbert expected, it was not this. I had the distinct pleasure of seeing him truly astounded, his pipe dangling forgotten from his hand. At last, he fumbled for a pair of tongs with which to light his pipe. Impulsively, I touched his sleeve. "Please don't," I said.

His expression darkened, but he tossed the pipe aside. "Tell me, then," he said in a growl, "how, exactly, gambling in a brothel will stop Masterson—"

"It's probably best if we don't explain," Jo interrupted. "Isn't that how this works? We know nothing about how you communicate with Mister Smith, and you, in turn, know nothing of our plans? So we cannot be used against each other."

"Of course," he muttered. "But I don't see why you need me."

"But surely you have been there. I suspect you might even be a regular—?" At his grimace, she smiled. "Exactly. So, it will be plausible for me to come in your company, rather than try and talk my way in." She leaned over and slapped his arm. "Mate."

He looked from her to myself and back again, his expression sullen now. "When do we have this merry outing?"

"You have to ask? The *Leviathan* sails this weekend, Captain. Masterson may not show tonight, but if he does …" She trailed off significantly.

But Captain Herbert was shaking his head. "That gives me no time to get approval."

"What do you need approval for?" I demanded.

"That this is worthwhile! Your job was to find evidence against Masterson. Nothing you find in a brothel will be taken seriously, while your presence will make a mockery of this entire enterprise. You will throw everything away with this little jaunt, but as it's clear you do not value my opinion, I will put it to Smith and let him dissuade you of this fancy."

I sensed Jo's rising anger and swiftly laid a hand on her knee, hidden beneath the table. "Sadly, we do not have time to wait for his opinion," I said. "You will have to trust us, otherwise we will simply proceed—though, if it is as you say, we might be best off taking our findings to Mister Smith directly? That way your conscience would be clear no matter the outcome."

He shifted uncomfortably in his seat. I kept the same bright smile on my face, kept my hand on Jo's flexing leg. At last, he exhaled dramatically and held out his hands.

"If you got yourselves killed, I would never forgive myself," he said.

Jo muttered something under her breath, but I kept the smile on my face. Inside, however, I realized that part of me was hoping he would balk. First an affirmative from Dr. Denham, and now this: for better or worse, we had a plan.

CHAPTER XI

An Unexpected Turn

Dr. Denham arrived soon after supper. True to his instructions, I was wearing an old apron over a plain dress. He carried a leather satchel and merely touched his hat. "Are you ready?"

I looked one last time at Jo, lovely in her best suit and wig. She winked at me from behind her spectacles. "Midnight in the kitchen, if I don't find you sooner."

I nodded. Part of me longed to kiss her goodbye, but I was aware of Dr. Denham's keen gaze, and instead gave her a little wave and went out into the icy night. Dr. Denham fell into step beside me. "I must say, when Mister Smith described your roles as unusual, he was putting it mildly."

"Circumstances require that we act as necessary, Doctor," I replied.

"Circumstances, it seems, have put two gentlewomen in the position of whore's nurse and libertine respectively." He shook his head. "What times we live in."

"Indeed, when men sell each other in chains, plot against their kings, and pay women pennies for their pleasures," I retorted. "Quite a time indeed."

The doctor pursed his lips, but thankfully changed the

topic. "When we arrive, Madame Viart may ask questions," he said after a moment. "She takes a keen interest in everyone who enters her establishment. I hope you have something plausible prepared."

"I cannot think I am the first woman to desire to help others," I said. "Is it that unusual?"

"Around here it is," the doctor said, gesturing at the little cottages. "For the wives of Medby, these women are a necessary evil, nothing more."

I was startled by this—startled and angered. I knew little of such things, but with our recent financial troubles and my own ambivalence to marriage, I might have found myself in difficult, perhaps dire circumstances. Would the wives of my village have shunned and scorned me in turn?

But I had more pressing matters to think on as we reached the door with its lanterns burning bright. We were admitted by a woman wearing only a thin petticoat and stays far too low for decency; though, of course, decency was not a concern here. Still, my face grew warm. I looked anywhere but at her powdered bosom. We entered a hall much like any house, with half-closed doors to either side. From within came laughter and voices, male and female alike. At the far end of the hall, a burly man, perhaps the brouette driver, watched us with disinterest.

"I'm making my rounds and I want to see Rose especially," the doctor explained. "Missus Read is assisting me," he added.

The girl led us up the stairs. It was just a house, I told myself, just a jumble of rooms like any house. As we ascended, the candlelight revealed just how sheer her petticoat was, how little it left to the imagination. I thought of Jo, who would arrive any time now: would she be greeted by the same woman? What of the years before she met me?

Lost in thought, I bumped into a man who gave me an indignant look. Flustered, I curtsied awkwardly. "My apologies," I managed.

He said nothing, only shouldered past me and disappeared around a far corner of the hall. He wore an expensive suit trimmed with gold braid, and red heeled shoes flashed beneath his clocked stockings.

"Owns a munitions factory," Dr. Denham said in my ear. "Scottish," he added.

"Where is he going?" I whispered.

"Upstairs. A private party hosted by one of our local merchants, Thomas Masterson."

Upstairs ... Afterwards, would he then retire to one of the rooms we were passing? The noises emanating from behind the doors left little to the imagination. At the end of the hall, we turned a corner and went down a few steps into a plainer wing. Here, we were led to a room with a simple bed, a washbasin, and a terrible chill, for the rusting stove was barely alight. The doctor frowned at this. "I told Madame Viart to keep this room warm," he said as he drew off his coat.

"Coal's expensive," the girl replied, walking out before we could press the matter. "I'll tell Rose you want her," she added over her shoulder.

Upstairs. But where would Thomas Masterson go afterwards? We would have to ascertain this first, and hopefully see inside before he retired with Madame Viart. We had several possible schemes for stealing the key, but they each relied on knowing the most plausible place where he would spend the night.

"What can I fetch?" I asked as Dr. Denham laid out his instruments.

"You mean, what excuse can I give you to go wandering? You can fetch me more water, if that would suit."

In the hall, a wan-faced young woman was approaching. At her startled expression, I touched her arm. "The doctor is waiting for you," I said reassuringly, moving past her and rounding the corner—

—only to backpedal at the sight of a man leaning against the balustrade at the top of the stairs.

Thomas Masterson.

Taking a deep breath, I cautiously peeked around the corner. The resemblance was even more striking at such close proximity. He was a younger, healthier copy of his brother, down to the haughty expression he wore. His plain wool suit, though well-made, was devoid of any ornament save a small brooch pinned to his chest.

A brooch like a strange sun, its rays undulating and its center hashed into triangles, for in truth, it showed the tentacles and teeth of the very antithesis of light.

"What is he thinking?" Mr. Masterson's voice was barely audible. "Of all the nights—the fool!"

I strained to hear further, but a voice whispered in my ear, "He is handsome, is he not?"

I turned to find the wan girl looking over my shoulder. Her shadowed eyes were alight with interest. "That's Mister Masterson," she told me. "Handsome *and* wealthy."

"The merchant?" I prompted.

"Well of course! And Madame keeps him all to herself," she added with a little toss of her head. "But who knows what will happen tomorrow."

I turned more completely. "Tomorrow?"

"There's a sailing party aboard his ship—surely you've seen the *Leviathan*?" She smiled then, a sly expression. "No wives allowed, I'm afraid."

For a moment I was confused, until I remembered that Dr. Denham had introduced me. "Just you and he?"

"I should be so lucky! No, there will be several of us, along with many prominent gentleman—even a vice-admiral." She winked at me. "Here's hoping Denham can patch me up. So many prospects, a girl can't be feeling poorly."

"Of course not," I murmured. She slipped away, but my heart was racing. Tomorrow, and several young women aboard? Oh, we were running out of time, and fast.

I looked again. Mr. Masterson was gone—but had he gone upstairs, or down to see the fool he spoke of? The munitions dealer had gone to the far side of the house, perhaps where more stairs lay. Downstairs, I could hear more voices now, all male, all rambunctious and laughing. Had the card game begun? Had Jo arrived?

It was not yet midnight and we needed a plan.

Swiftly, I moved along the landing to the far corner where the gentleman had disappeared. There was, indeed, a staircase just around the corner.

At the top of the stairs, lights were flickering. I crept up the first riser, then the next, straining to hear. There was a faint murmur of voices, a rumbling that at last separated into a rich, rolling cadence I knew all too well. I could not parse out the language, though I knew a little Latin and Greek. The syllables were harsh, each one a hammer blow to the ears. I imagined them being uttered commandingly to a dark sea, echoing through its depths to reach one particular listener.

Still, I crept up and up. It seemed Mr. Masterson was reciting a kind of prayer. As I reached the top of the stairs, he fell silent, and several other voices murmured in response.

"Thank you, gentlemen," he said. There was a door directly across from the stairs, with light gleaming at its base. "And now, to business."

I tiptoed towards the door as another man spoke, his words muffled. "That has been addressed," Mr. Masterson interrupted. "We are proceeding as planned. We sail tomorrow. The weather looks favorable, and once we are fully situated, we will make our demands."

Silently, I knelt at the door and peeked through the keyhole.

There was a table in the middle of the room with a half-dozen men crowded around it. I recognized Thomas Masterson by his suit alone, because they each wore a black mask that covered much of their faces, leaving only their mouths exposed. Embroidered on each mask, between the eyes, was the symbol of the beast wrought in golden thread.

On the table were several papers, including a map that Mr. Masterson was studying. Another man snatched up a smaller page and jabbed it at his fellows. "This is a copy!" he thundered. "Where is the original?"

"In my safekeeping," Mr. Masterson said. "We are in this

together, gentlemen, are we not? Surely, there can be no objection. Once our demands have been met, I will return each promissory note to its signatory, to keep or burn as they please."

The others muttered at this, but as he spoke, he pushed the map aside, tilting it towards the door. I squinted, trying to see—was that the coast of England or France?—when brisk footsteps clattered on the stairs below.

I did not think, I acted. I moved as swiftly as I could to the nearest open door, which turned out to be a small closet with a cistern. Here, I pressed myself against the cold, damp metal and closed the door, allowing for just a small space to peer through.

Then I had to smother my gasp, for the man who so jauntily ascended the stairs was none other than Captain Herbert.

He rapped on the door briskly, looking around as he did so. At once, Mr. Masterson appeared and pushed him down the hall, closing the door behind him. "What are you doing?" he demanded. "I told you to keep well away tonight."

"And I would have," Captain Herbert said, "but it seems I am about to perform another service for your cause, and I thought we should work out the payment in advance."

Mr. Masterson's mouth twisted. "Not here," he muttered. "I will meet you downstairs when I finish."

"Very well. But I would hurry, Tom." He smiled slyly. "We don't want any late obstacles, do we?"

He added something in French. I could not grasp the full meaning, but it sounded threatening, and to my untrained ear, remarkably fluent.

Mr. Masterson gave him a curt nod and returned to his

room, but Captain Herbert lingered, pacing up and down the little hall, his eyes raking over every door. "I don't know how it is you arrived before me, Miss Chase," he said. "I could have sworn I left you at the gaming table. But wouldn't it be better to hash this out, man to man?"

He laughed softly at the latter, but his hand was inside his coat, in all likelihood grasping a pistol. His eyes drifted downwards, still searching, and then alighted on the door I was hiding behind.

I looked down, and to my dismay and shame I saw the hem of my skirt had gotten caught in the opening.

His brow furrowed, and then he laughed again. "I think you best come out, Missus," he said, drawing a small pistol from inside his coat and pointing it at the door. "Remember, make a fuss and those gentlemen might hear, and they will do far worse to you than I."

My heart sank, but I remembered Mr. Windham's lessons. *Sometimes it's best to bide your time*, he had said. *Only a fool always takes the first opportunity.* I opened the door slowly, keeping my free hand up in the air.

"Ah, Missus," Captain Herbert purred. "I was wondering why your partner—sorry, your *husband*—was asking about the kitchen. Is that your rendezvous?" At my nod he gestured down the hall. "Then by all means, let us keep it."

He prodded me to another door, which opened to reveal a servants' stair. We descended, the pistol muzzle replacing the cold cistern against my back, all the more discomforting.

"I must say," he drawled as we descended, "your friend has much to learn about being a man. Letting you put yourself in danger while she plays whist? Not exactly the behavior of a gentleman. You should be safe and sound at home."

I bristled at this, but did not rise to the bait. *Heaven forbid I drive you to knit.*

We reached the basement, entering a warren of rooms. A larder, a room piled high with washing and mending, a servant's quarters, a room filled with casks of liquor, and at last, ahead, the glow of the kitchen hearth. Jo's back was turned to me and her hands raised. I could not think of how to warn her, and then Captain Herbert was shoving me through the door, grasping my arm to keep me close.

"I'm guessing we're right on time," he said, kicking the door closed behind us. "Now—"

Something moved behind him and I heard a meaty thud. The hand on my arm loosened and I twisted away while swinging my fist into his stomach, right where Mr. Windham had advised.

It hurt, more than I had anticipated, but I was rewarded with a satisfying cry of pain and the sight of Captain Herbert crumpling to the ground. Only then did I realize my blow was not his only injury, for his head was bleeding profusely. When I looked up, it was into yet another pistol muzzle, this one aimed unerringly at my face by none other than Madame Viart.

CHAPTER XII

Madame Viart

I was proud of myself for not panicking, and for the steadiness of my hands when I raised them. Jo moved closer to me, keeping her hands up. "Are you all right?" she asked.

"I think the captain has been lying," I said.

"Someone is certainly lying," Madame Viart said coolly. Her English was crisp and only slightly accented. "Exactly who remains to be seen."

"Surely you cannot still think us part of his scheme," Jo said. "He took Caroline prisoner!"

"That could have been a show—"

"How could he have known you followed me here?" A hint of exasperation was creeping into her voice. Turning to me, Jo continued grimly, "This little idiot is a French spy and she seems to think we're conspiring with Herbert and Masterson. But you're right about Herbert lying, Caroline—or perhaps we should call him Mister Hunt now, and ask him how he liked our village?"

I gaped at her. "How do you know?"

"We signed a guest book when we arrived tonight. It's the same bloody signature, I'd swear to it. I couldn't think what to do when I saw it, and then when he left, I went to find you. Only, this one was waiting for me." She gestured with annoyance at Madame Viart—an annoyance that I noted with relief, for had she believed the woman to be a true threat I knew she would be more circumspect.

"Wouldn't that make him another French spy?" I asked. "I heard him speaking French upstairs. He sounded fluent."

"Who was he speaking to?"

"Mister Masterson, though he called him 'Tom.' Apparently, he performed services for him and was about to do so again. Perhaps he meant you?"

"Probably." She nudged him with the toe of her boot. "Perhaps 'Mister Hunt' was a scheme of Masterson's? To make us think the French were involved?"

"Then we would focus our efforts on the French, leaving Mister Masterson free to act elsewhere," I agreed.

"I heard he was upstairs with some wealthy gentleman, including a shipyard owner—"

"I am still here," Madame Viart cut in irritably, "and I am still capable of shooting you."

"To what end?" Jo replied, while I said, "Surely we can avoid *that*."

"I have killed more than a dozen Englishmen—"

"All very deserving, I'm sure," Jo agreed. "But see it from our perspective, Madame. It is far more likely that *you* are conspiring with Captain Herbert, and the blow to the head was a show for *us*, to make us think otherwise."

I nodded. "That does make sense," I said to Madame Viart. "Although you hit him quite hard."

"You think I am working with him?" She stared at us,

astonished. "He is a sly, smug, bastard of a man, without loyalties or scruples. Yet, you think him my ally?"

"Isn't that what you're accusing us of?" I demanded.

"Look," Jo said firmly, putting her hand over Madame Viart's pistol. "Both our kings have stooped to using the likes of Captain Herbert or worse. That we would suspect each other of working with him is perfectly reasonable, but we are wasting time now. We must find out what Masterson plans to do tomorrow and stop it. You said the French are treating him as a threat—how?"

Madame Viart gave us each a keen look, then slowly lowered the gun, though she kept it primed and ready. "A flotilla has amassed at Calais and will engage Thomas should he make any attempt on us."

"But our navy might take that as provocation," Jo pointed out.

"Which is why I, and others, were tasked with finding out what he intends, and your government's complicity," she replied. "It may already be too late—he knows of the force at Calais, though I cannot think how. Perhaps through him," she added with distaste, waving her pistol at Captain Herbert.

"So, he has lured your ships close, and our navy is prepared for engagement ..." Jo trailed off significantly.

"And my girls will be at his side," Madame Viart said, a quiet fury in her voice. "He has held parties before with a girl or two, but this time he invited them all without asking me. He says he wants to fête his gentlemen properly." She was trembling now. "I will not be *used*, Mesdames. I will *serve*, but I will not be used, and I will not let my girls be used."

"To feed the beast," I said softly.

Jo was shaking her head. "You said he fed it anything—"

"And what better meal than a number of persons without families or influence?" As if on cue, Captain Herbert groaned at our feet. "Or a mercenary without loyalties?"

Madame Viart aimed the pistol at his head. "I should end him now—"

"No!" I smacked her hand away. "You cannot just shoot him!"

"If nothing else, it will bring them down upon us," Jo added, pointing at the ceiling.

"Hmph." She crossed her arms and pouted. For the first time that night, I really looked at her, at her rounded cleavage and the spots of color on her cheeks, how her hair looked exquisite even when tousled. A proper French spy, while I was dressed like an old maid.

"What do we do now?" Jo asked.

We eyed each other warily while Captain Herbert moaned and started to rise. Jo kicked him and he fell silent again.

"Will you help us in this?" I finally asked Madame Viart.

Her eyes flickered to mine where they held my gaze. The color of bluebells, a color I had always longed for.

"I can help you as a woman," she said. "A woman without a country. Do you understand?"

"You mean without fear of arrest," Jo said.

"I mean without the resources of France," she replied coldly. "My value to my country lies in my ears, what I can hear and report. If I *acted* in the name of my king they would simply discard me—and do you think England would treat you differently? We are women in a man's game; we are *nothing* compared to the fortunes of war. That is how I can help you—as a fellow nothing."

Jo looked at me, and I realized that she was waiting for me to speak. She was waiting for me to decide whether to trust this woman. What I wouldn't have given for a private room, just a few moments to compare our instincts—

But perhaps she was as hesitant as I.

"We need the key ring that Thomas Masterson carries," I said, surprised at my own calm voice. "Bring it to us and we can stop this."

Madame Viart eyed me. "That is all? A key ring will stop him?"

Jo started to speak, but I quickly said, "You will have to trust us, as we are trusting you."

"And if I cannot get it?"

"Then the *Leviathan* sails tomorrow with your ladies aboard and not a one will return."

She looked at Jo, who nodded firmly. "What Caroline says is true."

Slowly, she took a step to the door, then another. Her fingers flexed around the stock of the pistol, but she did not raise it again. As she opened the door, she nodded toward Captain Herbert. "What about him?"

"We'll secure him," Jo said.

"Hurry," I added. "We're running out of time."

With a final nod, she left. Jo drew the door nearly to, watching her, and then looked down at Captain Herbert. "Perhaps we should have let her kill him," she mused.

"Absolutely not!"

"He might have killed you," she pointed out, "and a man who would play countries against each other has few scruples, as she said."

"You seem to find her très sympathique," I snapped.

"You're being very protective of your captain."

"He's not—" I shook my head. "I thought you trusted my judgment," I said.

"When you are using your instincts," she amended, taking my hand. "What do they tell you about him?"

I looked down at his prone form. In his insensible state, all his bravado was gone. He was just another middle-aged man, tired and careworn. Like my father, long ago.

"I think he may come back to haunt us," I said slowly. "But I cannot justify his murder."

I waited for her to argue with me, but Jo only shrugged. "Then we better find something to secure him with," she said. "And another way out wouldn't hurt, in case she comes back with something larger than a key ring."

Jo rifled through the shelves then searched the hallway cabinets, coming up with a length of stout rope and a stubby knife. I tested the small windows near the top of the walls, tested the door at the far end of the kitchen. This was bolted, but at last I managed to work the door open. The icy gust made me shiver, but there were steps leading up to the outside—

And a padlocked iron gate.

"Not that way," I told Jo when I made my way back to her. She had tied Captain Herbert's hands and feet and was working her handkerchief into his mouth. He seemed to stir but otherwise did not respond. There was a great deal of blood on the stone floor. “What if he dies?” I asked.

“Then it will be his ghost haunting us,” she replied evenly.

I started to reach for him, thinking to stanch the flow of blood, but she caught my hand. “Caroline! We have much greater problems. If we have misjudged Viart, this doorway will be our only escape. We need to arm ourselves—or you could go now,” she said suddenly. “No, that’s better. I’ll stay to see what she chooses while you fetch help.”

“We are *not* separating,” I cut in. “There is no benefit in separating.”

“Save that you’ll be able to act.”

I folded my arms. “Then you leave and I’ll stay. You’re the better fighter, and you’ll have a better chance of reaching Mister Smith should we fail here.”

She gave me a look at once angry and miserable. I folded my arms and she folded hers in turn. “Caroline,” she said in a low voice, “if—if anything happened to you—”

“Do you think I feel any less about you?” I blurted out.

We both fell silent again, staring at each other. When the first tear wound its way down my cheek Jo wiped it away. Her own eyes were glistening.

“Then I suppose we better arm ourselves,” she said.

I swallowed. “Can I have the bigger knife?” I asked querulously. “Mister Windham says I am still too open when I fully extend my arm.”

“The biggest knife we can find, my darling,” she said, and the *my darling* warmed me as nothing ever had.

We found the kitchen knives easily enough, picking and

choosing among their hefts. The weight and sharpness of the blades quieted me. From the house above came the muffled sounds of laughter, singing; someone began playing a harpsichord. I kissed Jo's cheek impulsively and in turn she embraced me, our hands full of knives, large and small.

"Have I ever told you," she said in a sultry voice, "how becoming you look with a cleaver in your hand?"

"Even if I'm dressed like an old maid?" I asked, but I preened a little as I swished the blade one way and another.

"You are not old," Jo chided, kissing first my cheek, then the curve of my jaw.

"I am a spinster," I gasped. "On the shelf for good, now."

"Good," she said against my throat. "Spares you the attentions of every mooning stripling in Yorkshire."

"Mooning striplings aren't the worst fate," I breathed, for her lips were still stroking, pressing. "They at least flatter a woman when they woo her."

She raised her eyes to mine, and their expression made my stomach flutter. "Is that an invitation, Missus Read? Because you are already blushing in the most charming way—"

But she broke off as footsteps echoed in the hall. Together we moved into the shadows. I kept a long carving knife before me, the cleaver in my other hand, while Jo held two bright butcher's knives.

The door opened slowly, slowly—

To reveal Madame Viart, smiling triumphantly, a key ring held in her raised fist.

CHAPTER XIII

An Act of Theft

Madame Viart would not say exactly how she secured the key ring, but she hinted enough that even I grasped the implication. Jo finally silenced her with a curt, "Yes, yes, you are the most skilled lover in the world, well done." Her exasperation was a balm upon my jealousy, for if anything, Madame Viart had returned even more flushed, tousled, and lovely. How could one woman look that beautiful?

I had no time to think on it, though. She assured us she could keep Mr. Masterson occupied for a few more hours, but it would be morning soon and he was eager to oversee the *Leviathan*'s preparations. Thus, when we left the brothel, we did not return home, but instead made our way straight to the waterfront, Jo's collar turned up to obscure her face and my hood pulled low. Halfway there, we found ourselves enveloped in a thick white fog. We descended into it as swimmers descending into an icy lake, our pace slowed by the lack of visibility. By the time we reached the bay, we could barely make out the outlines of the buildings and were reduced to inching forward. What time was it? I longed to see the horizon, but I could barely see past Jo's back. I kept touching the knife in my pocket.

"Jo," I whispered. "Jo, if there's nothing in the cabinet—"

"Then we will think of another plan," she said firmly.

"It's nearly morning—"

"Cabinet," she said in the same firm tone. Then, over her shoulder: "You know the mood here, how everyone looks up to him. We have to find proof of his treason first. Everything else must wait."

There was no more opportunity to argue then, for Mr. Masterson's company was just ahead of us. The building seemed deserted, its shutters closed and the lamp above the door unlit. We pressed against a nearby building, straining to see into the fog, but the air around us was still and silent. Other than the brothel denizens, all of Medby seemed to have retired for the night.

Taking my icy hand in hers, Jo led me not to the entrance, but between the buildings, until we reached a ginnel. Here, we tiptoed to a nondescript back door. "I fixed the bolt earlier," Jo whispered. "Hopefully no one noticed."

I pressed close to the wall as she bent over the doorknob, using her knife to coax the latch open. In the ginnel, the fog was, impossibly, more dense, completely erasing the buildings to either side. The smallest noises made me jerk with anticipation. At any moment I expected to see Mr. Masterson or Mr. Morrow hurtling towards us. My chest hurt from my heart beating, beating—

—but then the door swung open noiselessly and Jo was beside me once more. "Oiled the hinges," she breathed, a hint of pride in her voice. "Let's see just what Thomas Masterson is hiding."

We entered the building, crowding together in utter darkness as Jo worked the door closed again. She moved away from me and I felt a new kind of panic, the same as when we were lost in the tunnels beneath Harkworth Hall. Then, we had emerged to find ourselves between a monster and a madman. What awaited us this time?

A tinder sparked, then settled into the warm glow of a candle. Jo raised it in the air and I saw we were in a large room lined with shelves, as if to store items … save that there were only a few small crates in one corner. Jo waved me to the nearest one and raised the lid. Inside was a pile of plain woolen coats, all of a deep blue color.

"The same color as naval uniforms—French and English," she said.

"Hedging his bets?" I touched one, wondering at how such a simple garment could be so loaded with deadly possibility.

"Indeed, and if we give our navy wrong information, it could prove disastrous." She led me up a few rickety stairs and through a heavy wooden door. On the other side was a tastefully decorated hall leading to the main entrance. The floor was a plain, battered parquet, but the walls were covered with flocked paper and a polished wainscoting, with fine sconces lining the hall. On either side were two rooms crammed with desks and chairs, ornamented by framed maps of shipping routes. Still Jo did not pause, but led me up a more formal staircase. As we ascended, the candlelight slowly revealed, inch by inch, a painting hung halfway up.

At first glance, it was nothing more than a family portrait

with a father, mother, and two boys on a hillside. They stood in the shade of a spreading oak tree, a red rose unnaturally vivid in the father's lapel. Despite the youth of the boys, the resemblance to Edward and Thomas Masterson was plainly apparent. Behind the hill lay open sea running to a blue horizon. The whole of the painting seemed to ripple as we climbed the stairs. There was something about the play of texture and light that made it seem unnaturally alive.

Jo had noticed as well and slowed her pace. She waved the candle one way and another, then went perfectly still.

The painting rippled again, though the light was now fixed, and my stomach vanished. "Let's find those papers and go," I whispered.

My words seemed to rouse her. She shook herself and we hurried up the stairs. We entered an office so devoid of character as to seem abandoned, save for the half-burned candles and the dark ink on the blotter. Jo gestured for me to close the door while she went to a large, plain cabinet and fitted the key to the lock. For one terrible moment it would not turn. My belly lurched again while Jo cursed under her breath, but with a snap it finally rotated and the cabinet doors opened wide.

Inside were two shelves of ledgers in neat stacks, but Jo was peering worriedly at the empty bottom shelf. "That wallet was here," she said in a low voice. "I swear I saw it just today. But if he moved it, it could be anywhere."

I moved next to her and crouched down, studying the cabinet shelf, then felt carefully inside. There was a narrow lip of wood that ran on all three sides, but near the back I found what I was looking for. I could not help smiling smugly as I pressed the little button. The shelf snapped up, revealing a tray underneath—and the leather wallet, clearly marked with the radiating symbol of the beast.

"My father's desk has a secret drawer," I admitted at her astonished look. "He used to hide the overdue bills inside it."

She looked at me a moment longer, then kissed me with such ferocity I gasped. When we broke apart we both started to speak, then stopped. I laid my hand on the curve of her cheek, flushed now with excitement. Then, as if of one mind, we turned and lifted out the leather bundle, laid it on the desk, and drew out the papers.

Thomas Masterson's hand was so small as to be illegible at times, but a broad understanding soon emerged. Here were promissory notes with seals testifying to their authenticity, many for titled names. Here were vast sums in banks in London, Paris, and Florence. A deed for a fashionable Mayfair house. Several pages of ancestral genealogies. The latter drew my attention, but before I could parse their meaning, Jo spread out a map of the eastern coast of England with many pencil marks overlaid. At the mouth of the Thames was drawn a small, undulating shape that we knew far too well.

"He's blockading the Thames," Jo murmured. There was a reverence in her voice that I instinctively understood. This was not a display of bravado at a foreign power; this was an attempt to suffocate the very heart of England. The tiny, penciled shape seemed almost obscene.

"If he sails tomorrow, he'll arrive in a few days," she continued. "And if the Navy is distracted by the French fleet at Calais …"

"Or directed to that distraction," I put in. "Rose, at the brothel, she said he counts a vice-admiral among his friends."

"Bloody hell." Jo thumbed through the remaining papers, her frown deepening. "We have to get this to Smith—"

But we both went still and silent as cold air blew over us, making the candle flicker—a draft where there had been no draft before.

And then, downstairs, a faint creak.

Jo stuffed the papers back in the wallet and shoved it in my arms. "Go into the hall and turn right," she whispered, then blew out the candle. As I inched my way to the door I heard the the shelf snap in place.

"What are you doing?" I whispered.

"Hallway window," she replied, shoving me forward. I eased the door open and tried to use the dim light to see what Jo was doing. Now, books were being piled on the desk.

"Jo?"

"If they think we only saw the accounts, it might buy us time," she whispered. "Go! I'm right behind you."

I heard a male voice somewhere below, a single syllable. I did as I was told. Turning right led me to a shuttered window at the end of the hall, which opened to reveal a roof below me, and beyond it, the ginnel. Without waiting, I shoved the window open and swung myself onto the sill. Jo appeared, tucking the wallet under her arm as she helped me climb down onto the roof. When my feet found purchase on the slate, I reached up to receive her, but instead found myself catching the wallet.

"Run," Jo said as she swung a leg over the sill. "They can't chase us both, I'll distract them as much as I can." When I only stood there, suddenly rigid with fear, she gave me a strained smile. "Do your duty, country girl."

I looked at her one last time. The moonlight etched every detail of her beautiful face in my mind. She seemed more real than anything I had ever seen before or would see again.

I looked, then turned and skidded to the far side of the roof. There I sat on the edge and then dropped into the ginnel below, the wallet clutched to my chest. Fog rippled and pooled around me like cold water. From inside the building, I heard footsteps rushing towards me, many and loud, and without daring to look up, I ran.

I skidded down the ginnel until I reached an intersection. I could not go back the way we had come, yet I was running away from the landmarks I knew. I paused, but there were feet ringing out on the cobblestones behind me. I turned and made for the bay.

Once I reached the waterfront, however, I again felt disoriented. I ducked into a doorway, trying to think: to go home now would have me walking directly past Mr. Masterson's building, but any other direction would bring me back into fog-filled alleys and ginnels where who knew how many were searching.

I wedged the wallet under my arm and covered all with my cloak, then turned right and began inching my way back towards Mr. Masterson's company. The mist swirled around my skirts like eddies in water. Was I leaving a trail behind me? I heard footsteps, sensed someone else close by. Ahead of me, the door to Mr. Masterson's company opened—

—and behind me a light suddenly appeared in the fog, a hazy spot that coalesced into a tall man swinging a lantern gaily as he tested each door he passed.

The watchman.

"Sir!" I gasped, reaching for him. His startled expression softened as he took in my stricken expression. "Oh thank God! I am completely lost."

"What are you doing out at this hour?" He looked around me. "Good God! Don't you know it's well past curfew?

"My father is sick," I babbled, sensing someone approaching. "I was looking for Doctor Denham's house, but the fog confused me. I thought to follow the bay, but it's worse down here—only my father is terribly feverish, I fear for his life!"

I clutched at his sleeve, my honest fear giving credence to my story. The watchman nodded, then his face darkened and he raised the lantern, peering at the darkness behind me. "Who goes there?" he barked.

There was only silence, yet I had the distinct feeling of being observed.

"Odd, I thought I heard something." The watchman shook himself. "Doctor Denham, you say? He's down at the other end, Miss."

"Oh no," I gasped.

The watchman sighed. "Come on, then," he said, taking my arm. "Though you're trouble for my schedule."

We began walking inland, following the curve of the

buildings. As we drew close to Mr. Masterson's company, I saw movement out front that soon revealed itself to be three men: Mr. Morrow and two large men in greatcoats. I twitched the hood of my cloak further over my face and pressed close to the watchman.

"What's this?" he demanded, raising his lantern high. "Do you have permission to be out here?"

"We do," said Mr. Morrow, drawing out a paper from his pocket. He stepped in front of us, blocking the watchman's view of the door, and held it up while the watchman peered at it.

He had not, however, blocked my view. One of the men yanked Jo out of the door and pushed her towards the beach. Her hands were together in front of her, a coat tossed over them, hiding some kind of bonds; her face was mottled with bruises. It was all I could do to keep from crying out. She did not so much as glance at me. My throat was pin-tight and tears slipped out despite my efforts.

"Very well," the watchman huffed. "Though I wish we would be told about these things. Another fellow might have tried to give you a thrashing!"

"My apologies," Mr. Morrow said. His eyes flickered over me, but he merely continued. "I will be sure to inform you the next time we have an … inventory problem."

There was a hint of slyness in his voice that made my hackles rise, but the watchman patted my hand. "Well," he said. "Must be getting on, the lady needs a doctor."

"Then I will delay you no further," Mr. Morrow said, stepping aside. "I hope you are soon restored, Miss," he added.

The slyness, the sound of a boat being pushed into the water—oh, I was nearly overcome by a riot of emotions. It was all I could do to keep pace with the watchman. What would they do with her? I could think of only one reason to bring her to the *Leviathan* and it made my blood run cold.

Do your duty, country girl.

"That's Mister Masterson's crew," the watchman explained, patting my hand. "They do insist on doing so much at night! Still, a fine man, Mister Masterson. He's bought a frigate just to protect us from the French! More than George has ever done for us, I must say. Why, his navy hardly goes north of Yarmouth, though he's happy to tax us for it."

I merely nodded, for I did not trust myself to speak. Would they move forward their plans now? Was Thomas Masterson still at the brothel? How much time did I have?

"If there were any justice in the world," the watchman went on, "I reckon it would be Mister Masterson heading our navy."

I swallowed my bitter laugh. Oh, that would be a fine world indeed, with the Royal Navy consigning bodies to feed a monster. But, in truth, I could not see Mr. Masterson engaging in such work, even at the highest rank. The power he craved was something far more passive, I suspected—and lucrative.

We had reached the far end of the waterfront. Now we ascended a familiar little street: here was the edge of the market, here the sign for the coach road, and at last, the squat brown home of Dr. Denham was before me. I started to pull away, thanking the watchman, but he patted my hand again.

"I'd be a sorry fellow to bring you all this way, only to see you robbed on the Doctor's doorstep! I'm not going until I see you safely inside."

My heart sank, but there was nothing for it. Was he even back from the brothel? I knocked vigorously, smiling at the watchman, and waited. I heard muffled footsteps and a grumbling voice, and a servant opened the door.

"Back so soon, Miss?" he began, frowning. "Or did he—"

"I know we were here earlier," I interrupted swiftly, angling my head at the watchman. "But my father is terribly ill, I was hoping the Doctor might come. Is he available?"

Thankfully the servant was quick-witted. His expression became apologetic. "I'm afraid he's out visiting a patient," he said.

"Then perhaps I can wait for him?" I stepped into the doorway before the servant could reply and inclined my head at the watchman. "Thank you again for all your kindness."

"Miss," he said, touching his hat. "I hope he comes back soon, for your father's sake."

The servant made to shut the door, but I took the knob myself and closed it only partway. From there, I watched until the watchman finally turned a corner to cut back down to the bay. As soon as he was out of sight I opened the door once more.

"My apologies," I said to the servant. "Please thank your master for the use of his vestibule, especially at such an hour."

"Is he all right?" the servant asked, looking nonplussed.

"I left him in fine fettle," I confirmed. "Only I, ah, I had to fetch something, and I was caught out after curfew. I did not want to arouse suspicion." I was already inching my way out. "Again, please thank him for me," I repeated.

Before the man could question me further, I darted into the street, now clutching the precious wallet to my chest. The cobblestones were slippery with frost, but still I walked as fast as I could, running on the muddier stretches, able to think only of getting home, the better to reason out how to get Jo back.

PART III

Leviathan

CHAPTER XIV

A Rescue

"Masterson's mad," Mr. Simmons said.

We were crowded around the table of the little cottage. Mr. Simmons was dressed, but my father was swathed in blankets over his greatcoat over his banyan. I had hoped to let him sleep, but he had insisted on joining us. For far too long, we had studied the papers from Thomas Masterson's cabinet, with periodic interruptions as Mr. Simmons climbed the hill behind our house and confirmed that yes, the *Leviathan* was still there, its masts jutting tall and dark from the swirling mist.

At last, we were faced with the complete truth. In addition to what Jo and I had seen, there were lists of men's names from across the North with their age and skills, and a list of ships, their owners, and how many bodies they could transport. The map of the coast, Mr. Simmons believed, showed naval dockyards and patrols all the way from Medby to Greenwich, and possibly the positions of allies. There were brief missives in French and Dutch, which promised sums of money and additional men, in exchange for favorable terms in trade and territory.

And there was that undulating shape, limned at the mouth of the Thames and seeming to span its entirety.

"It's a big beast," Mr. Simmons continued. "But it's not big enough to block the river."

"It's enough if he has help," I said, tapping the list of ships. "And if there are those in government who favor his cause."

"A coup," my father proffered, his eyes gleaming.

"There's no royal connection in those ancestry charts," I pointed out.

"I don't think he wants the throne," Mr. Simmons opined. "Just a title and maybe a nice, rich colony to go with it. All those foreign promises are about trade, not treaties."

"Meanwhile, the French will attack at the slightest provocation," I said, looking out the window. With the sunrise, I could just glimpse the bay and its harbor, though I could not see the *Leviathan*'s masts. I wanted nothing more than to run to that ship and free Jo—or at least share in her fate. Her absence felt a deep, physical ache, bordering on a depth of grief I did not want to consider. But that was my heart; I also had a duty, as she had reminded me.

"I have to get these papers to Grimsby," I said. "Mister Windham is there, as is the Navy. They need to know of this."

Mr. Simmons and my father exchanged a look. "I can go to Grimsby, Miss," Mr. Simmons said. "Mister Windham knows me as well as you."

"Better him," my father said, tapping his face.

"There's a chance you might be recognized, if Captain Herbert had accomplices," Mr. Simmons explained.

"Mister Simmons," I began in a low voice. "I appreciate

your concerns for my safety, but I cannot sit around here waiting—"

"Not sit," my father interrupted, pointing at the window. "Go."

"To the *Leviathan*," Mr. Simmons said, "to try to stop that ship."

I stared at them, my mouth dropping open in my astonishment.

"We had already talked about what might happen should we have to send for Mister Windham ourselves, you see," Mr. Simmons continued. "So, we planned that I would ride there, and your father would fall upon the sword and place himself in Missus Lambert's company."

I had closed my mouth; now it dropped open again. "Why her?" I asked.

My father sighed mournfully. "Keep watch," he said.

"Her sister owns one of the alehouses along the harbor," Mr. Simmons explained, ignoring my father's furious look. "Not far from Masterson's company, as it happens. He can keep watch there, make sure our fellow doesn't suddenly change his plans."

As he spoke I saw, all in a rush, how it might work—how it *could* work, if the three of us acted in concert.

"So, you are to ride with all haste to Grimsby, I am to try to stop a ship from attacking our capital, and my father is to … drink?" But even as I spoke, my eyes were filling.

"I think that's about right," Mr. Simmons said with a grin.

I looked at my father and was surprised to see his eyes glistening as well. He leaned over and took my hand. Mr. Simmons muttered something about coal and left the room.

"You are happy," he said, speaking carefully. "With her."

I nodded. I was weeping now. My father wiped my tears, the feel of his touch so familiar, it made me cry harder.

"Bring her home," he whispered. "*Safe*."

Before I knew what I was doing, I was beside him, hugging him. "My girl," he said, his voice thick. "My girl." When I drew away, he too was weeping. He kissed my cheek and I his. From the doorway, Mr. Simmons coughed, and then there was nothing more to say, for it was morning and there was no more time. I left them to organize themselves and went upstairs to change, wiping my face and breathing deeply to calm myself. This was no time for tears—or dresses. Still, I felt my father's touch upon my face, like a kind of benediction.

If only Mr. Windham could have seen me, in Jo's plain suit, my limbs suitably free for violence. I carried two pistols, as if I were some kind of brigand; in each boot was a knife, my own and another slender blade that Mr. Simmons silently gave me. I hesitated over my note to Madame Viart as he dressed my father, unsure of what tone to take—I had need of her again, but little to offer her by recompense. In the end, I simply stated my need and prayed. Then Mr. Simmons was gone with both note and wallet, and my father and I were alone.

"Let's," he said.

For the first time, I appreciated just how nuanced my

father's speech had become, for I heard a dozen shades of emotion in that one utterance. For the first time, as well, I realized I might never see him again. Without speaking, I helped him into his heavy coat and donned my cloak over Jo's suit. As we left, he took our old spyglass and slipped it into his pocket.

Outside, it was bitterly cold and my father pressed closer to me, like a child. We struggled towards Mrs. Lambert's door. Surreptitiously, I inhaled over and over, trying to hold within me his smell, that animal scent I had known all my life.

I might never see him again.

Mrs. Lambert threw open the door as we reached her threshold, so that we did not even have a moment for our parting. I could not tell if I was relieved or hurt, that my father ducked inside so quickly. For one brief moment she was utterly silent as she took in my legs. Then her need to chatter got the better of her, and she began prattling away as I stomped my feet and tried to get a word of goodbye in. I became attentive, however, when she asked me if I would fetch my father after the celebration.

"What celebration?" I asked.

"Why, the *Leviathan* sails today," she declared. "And the French have been spotted in the Channel, so they may even come back with heads upon pikes. Wouldn't that be a sight?" She grinned ghoulishly at the prospect. "Meanwhile, it's free beer for an hour before she sails, and cakes for the little ones."

I blinked, once again astonished at the audacity of Mr. Masterson's plans. It was not enough to sally forth and extort England, he would do so with all of Medby cheering him on.

"My sister will have a table all ready for us, right at the window so we can watch without catching our deaths." She patted my father's arm. "You should join us as soon as you finish your errands! Everyone will be there, even the vicar, and poor Missus Perkins might even leave her sickbed—"

I cut into what promised to be a long list of Medby's citizenry with heartfelt thanks and a wave at my father. He merely nodded once, his eyes red, before disappearing into her snug cottage. I could hear her voice halfway down the street—my poor father! His patience would be sorely tried. He would take much cosseting when we returned.

If we returned.

It had been mere hours since we left the brothel, but in the morning light, it looked a different place entirely. What had seemed like a dark maze of rooms and halls revealed itself to be a simple house, larger than its neighbors, but otherwise unremarkable. There were even lace curtains in the windows above the iced-over flower boxes.

Before I could knock, Madame Viart swept outside, as if she had been watching for me. Behind her, a half-dozen women followed like a gaggle of cloaked geese, huddling together as they loudly protested both the hour and the cold.

"Silence!" Madame Viart barked, then looked me over. "For a moment I thought you were the other one," she remarked. "Do you both wear breeches? Surely that complicates—"

"You've done as I asked?" I interrupted. My voice was

trembling with fear and impatience. Every hour, they could be hurting Jo more …

But they had kept her alive when they could have easily killed her, and she was valuable to Thomas Masterson in at least one way: as food for his monster.

“Perhaps.” Madame Viart drew me aside, tucking her arm into mine. “You did not say, Madame, what you would do for me in return?”

“What do you want?” I winced at the desperation in my voice. *Anything*, my heart cried out. *Anything, if you would just get me on that ship*.

“Oh, I cannot think of anything *now*,” she said, pursing her lips. “Just as long as I can ask for something in time. Think of it as an unwritten promissory note? From you to me, no one else involved. Yes?”

I looked at her pristine face with its rouged lips, the velvet mouche in the corner of her dimpled cheek. As pretty as a doll, and, I suspected, with as much heart. “Yes,” I said.

“Good.” She beamed at me as if I were a prize pupil. “Everything is better between women,” she said with satisfaction.

“What of Captain Herbert?”

“Tied in my cellars. I will think of something.” She waved her hand airily. “And look! Our transportation has arrived. Thomas will be pleased I roused myself so early.”

“Pleased or suspicious?” I eyed the two vehicles coming towards us: an elegant carriage, and a most inelegant cart bearing several large barrels. Even in the icy air I caught the smell of blood.

“Pleased, of course. He thinks all I know are fucking and

jewelry." She rattled off the words. "Though, if he does suspect, rest assured I will see your throat cut before my own." Before I could respond to this, she waved the cart driver to us. "Six and one empty, yes?"

"Yes, Miss." The man climbed down from his perch, clearly unsure where to look, for even in the cold Madame Viart chose to display her décolletage. I felt a pang of sympathy.

"Excellent. Put her in the empty one." And with a last, imperious wave she strode off to the carriage.

Never had I been so thankful for my small stature. Had I been the size of Mr. Windham, or even my father, our ruse could never have happened. What had seemed like a vast container from without suddenly became as narrow as a pinhole when I was faced with inserting myself into it. I had to divest myself of my cloak, and when I wiggled completely inside, I was folded so tightly I struggled to breathe, my arms forced atop my head.

"All right?" the man said, and without waiting for my reply, tapped the lid into place. Thankfully, he did not nail it shut or I might have lost all nerve. Besides my snug cage, there was the scent of the other barrels, stronger now that I was among them. I fancied I could hear dripping sounds. Six barrels of fresh offal. Another mark on my tally sheet with Madame Viart, and what might she ask for in return?

But there was no point in worrying about that now. Instead, I thought of Jo and where I was bound. My first task would be to find her, and to ascertain how badly she had been hurt. Her bruised face filled my mind and I wept again to think of it. But she had walked out of the office without any visible injury; perhaps they had done what they deemed necessary to overpower her and no more.

It seemed an age before the cart finally lurched forward. My arms were already starting to tingle, and now there was every rut and bump in the road to contend with. With every rattle I slipped incrementally lower. What if I could get no leverage to escape? What if they flung the barrels overboard before we could enact our plan? What if …

My dark thoughts, however, were interrupted by a murmuring sound that grew louder as we approached it, separating into a cacophony of voices. The cart driver began shouting for people to get out of the way. I could not see, but I could imagine the crowd that would be gathering at the water's edge, eager to partake of Thomas Masterson's generosity. A few men were singing shanties and a woman was yelling that it was damn cold and where were the cakes? Hands slapped the cart's sides and someone struck my barrel, demanding rum, so startling me that I had to smother my cry. A heated argument broke out and I feared what might happen should they force my hiding place open, but then I heard a calm voice that quelled the noise around me.

"What's this, then?" Mr. Morrow said.

"Missus Viart's request," the cart driver replied. In his mouth her name became *vart*, a variation I suspected she would not appreciate. "She wants to make some kind of Frenchie stew? Those people will eat anything," he added.

"So I've been told." The cart rocked as Mr. Morrow climbed aboard—for I was certain it was him, so close was his voice. He sniffed one barrel after another and I heard him wrench open the one next to me. My arms were numb, how could I get to my weapons—

"Fuck me," a man opined. "Is it all innards?"

"You can keep that, Joe," another put in with a laugh.

I sensed Mr. Morrow standing over me, considering. He tapped the lid back into place, and then his knuckles rapped my own. I clenched my eyes shut as he rocked my barrel back and forth experimentally. Any moment now. Any moment the lid would come off, and then—?

But suddenly the cart rocked again. "Have them taken out to the *Leviathan*," Mr. Morrow said, his voice farther away. "Straight into the hold. I will see to them myself once everything is aboard."

And with that ominous promise, I was in.

CHAPTER XV

Monsters

They dropped me without ceremony onto a boat which lurched and rolled on the choppy water. Nearby, a man muttered about weather coming in. Just as I feared I might be sick, I was hoisted into the air, swung wildly about, and then dropped, causing me to nearly bite my tongue off with the jarring impact. When at last I stopped moving, all I could taste was bile and I feared I might never use my arms again. But I was on board. Jo had to be nearby, and once I freed her we would flee, back to my father and Mr. Simmons, back *home*. The thought made tears rush to my eyes, like a homesick child.

But I was no child anymore, and we had much to overcome.

Every time I started to push myself upwards there were footsteps. Where had I been placed? I had a vision of myself popping out of the barrel to find myself in a throng of Mr. Masterson's men. If only Madame Viart would come—but perhaps Madame Viart could not come; perhaps Madame Viart did not care to come. She had completed her task and gotten me on board. She had given me no assurances of further aid.

At last, the hold fell silent and remained so. I could hear the faint sounds of a voice bellowing, punctuated by cheers—perhaps Mr. Masterson was making a speech? If so, now was my opportunity. My knees and hips ached as I pushed up, my limp arms pressing against the lid of the barrel until I heard a popping sound and the lid came free.

Slowly, I stood up, blinking at the bright sunlight that streamed in through the portholes. I was wedged among the other barrels, and other casks and crates besides: I recognized the branded symbol and LEVIATHAN from the crates at Harkworth Hall. More arms, or uniforms? Or more food for his living weapon? Not that it mattered now. The only thing that mattered was Jo.

I stood up completely, pushing the lid atop another barrel to keep it from clattering to the floor. My arms exploded into a thousand excruciating pinpricks, hanging limp and useless as I tried to work my legs free. I willed my fingers to coil, willed my arms to move, but was rewarded with only the slightest movement. It was all taking too long—

Footsteps descended from above and I panicked. I could not return to my hiding place; all I could do was brace myself against another barrel and pull my legs out, dragging myself atop the casks with my fingers tangling into awkward fists. My feet came free as a shadow cut across my vision. I seized one pistol and held it, though I could not fit my forefinger into the trigger.

There was a faint gunshot outside, cries and raucous laughter rising up in its wake. The shadow stumbled at the sound, the hood of its cloak slipping down, and I found myself staring at an angry Madame Viart. "You!" she cried. "I would speak with you, Madame. Your idiot plan will not work!"

I slid off the cask, relieved when my legs did not collapse beneath me. My hand tightened properly around the pistol, the shape of the trigger comforting against my finger. "Where is Jo?" I demanded.

"What does it matter? We cannot leave. Have you a plan for that?"

"What do you mean, we cannot leave?"

She drew close to me and the rage in her eyes made me flinch. "There are no other boats," she hissed at me. "No—oh, what do you say, jollies? The little boats. They have all rowed back to Medby."

I gaped at her, my confusion giving way to a horrible sinking feeling. I had not thought, I had not thought. We were trapped.

"We are trapped here," Madame Viart continued, as if she could read my very thoughts. "I asked Thomas about the little boats, and he said we are going for a short journey, what do we need of little boats?" She seized the lapels of my coat. "You said we would not die here, you said all we had to do was throw the barrels over and flee. But we cannot flee!"

I opened my mouth to say—something, anything—but what came out was the voice of a man.

"How very true, Madame," Captain Herbert drawled. He stepped forward from the shadows, pointing a pistol at us. "All the better for me."

I whirled about, aiming my own pistol, but Captain Herbert merely smiled. "I think I prefer you in the breeches, Miss Daniels." His hair was matted with blood and a purple bruise had swollen near his hairline; still, he had found time to change his coat for a clean one. "Tom will enjoy meeting you. A matching set of harpies: a fine gift for his pet squid."

"I am no harpy," Madame Viart said haughtily.

"Where is Jo?" I asked, priming my pistol.

"Do you really want to find out which of us shoots faster?" Captain Herbert shrugged. "I've spent my entire youth on battlefields, Miss Daniels. You'll be dead before your shot reaches me, I can assure you."

"Oh yes, the great soldier," Madame Viart retorted. "A vulture picking corpses."

"When I finish with the Englishwomen," Captain Herbert said, "I'm going to gut you like a fish, Viart."

"Sir!" I blurted out. "There is no need."

"Indeed, there is not," another voice said.

We all turned once more, to see Mr. Morrow standing with four men on the stairs, two of them with pistols drawn. I should have been more frightened, but my fear was giving way to frustration. All I wanted was to be taken to Jo, even if it meant being taken prisoner.

"Mister Masterson is concerned that you would board his ship without telling him, Mister Hunt," Mr. Morrow continued. "I have been asked to take you to him."

"These women are plotting against you," Captain Herbert said furiously. "They plan to rouse the monster and escape."

"I thought that was everyone's plan, Mister Hunt," Mr.

Morrow replied. He nodded to his men. "Disarm them all, and one of you take Mister Hunt to see Mister Masterson."

"But the women—" Captain Herbert began.

"I will put them where they belong," Mr. Morrow said. "I would not delay, Mister Hunt. There is much talk upstairs about percentages ...?"

He trailed off significantly. I could see the indecision playing over Captain Herbert's gaunt features as he weighed profit against revenge. At last, his pistol lowered, and one of Mr. Morrow's men relieved him of it and nudged him up the stairs while another patted me down. I handed my pistol over without protest, for what was the use? The ship was filled with men loyal to Mr. Masterson. The man quickly extracted my other pistol, and the knife from my boot—

—but he missed Mr. Simmons' little dagger.

As he slid his hands up and down my legs I looked witheringly at Mr. Morrow. "Is this necessary?"

"Dress like a man, get treated like a man," Mr. Morrow replied.

Another man was trying, and failing, to see under Madame Viart's cloak; she kept smacking at his hands, her face a mask of fury. "That is *satin* you are pawing," she snapped.

But Mr. Morrow paid her no mind. He had opened one of the barrels again, staring inside as if he could divine some meaning from the bloody shapes. At last he nodded. "Cutler, take the women upstairs. You two, help me throw these overboard."

"No!" I cried out. Madame Viart hissed in disapproval as the four men looked at me, Mr. Morrow's mouth twitching at the corners.

"This meat is not fit for consumption," Mr. Morrow said. "It may be the basis of some French delicacy, but if so, it's too delicate for us." He nodded to his men. "We'll throw it out the back; I don't want our guests to see."

"But—" I tried frantically to think of what might dissuade him. "We're still close to shore," I began. Close to shore, and my father was at the harbor, along with so many others—

But his gaze met mine and I saw something new in his eyes: something calculating.

"Exactly, Miss Daniels," he said, and pointed at the stairs.

A pistol prodded me into step behind Madame Viart. Many things seemed to happen at once, then. I was trying to think of how to stop him, even as the men began rolling the barrels towards the back of the ship. A loud, metallic rattling told me the anchor was being raised, the ship creaking as if eager to leap forward. The crowd cheered, and more pistols snapped—

—and beneath it all, a low voice began speaking, reciting strange yet familiar syllables. I froze halfway up the stairs, ignoring his man's snarl. "You're calling it," I gasped. "You're calling it here, now—but *why*?"

Mr. Morrow's gaze met mine again: calculating, unfathomable. "Upstairs," he said, and I was shoved into daylight.

We were prodded and steered across a deck crowded with men—so many men. There were sailors racing up and down the rigging like rats, dashing one way and another as they checked lines and sails, measured wind and called out orders. Their movements were hampered, though, by all the other men: farmers and workers bundled against the cold and armed with everything from rifles to axes, interspersed with gentlemen resplendent in fur-trimmed greatcoats and carrying glasses of liquor. It was a strange sight, a tableau of many kinds of anger all gathered together, all temporarily united in one cause.

Of Captain Herbert, I saw no sign, but as we were propelled towards the stern I saw Thomas Masterson striding towards us, and for the first time he *saw* me, truly saw me. The man was alight with excitement. If he heard the faint, steady plopping of the barrels he made no sign. I glanced one last time at Medby, its beach crowded with bodies, some waving flags of England. It was a heartbreaking sight. They were singing in full-throated unison

Am I a soldier of the cross,
a foll'wer of the Lamb?
And shall I fear to own His cause
or blush to speak His Name?

That, Thomas Masterson heard, and it made him smile.

"Wait," he said as we drew near. "I would see the woman who killed my brother."

At that ridiculous pronouncement, I couldn't help but laugh. "I never so exerted myself, sir," I said. "Your brother was eaten by his hubris. I did not need to lift a finger."

If my words had any effect on him, he masked his emotions perfectly. "Put her in the room with the other one," he told our guard. "I want to give the Madame a personal tour—"

He was interrupted, however, by a thin, echoing wail that I felt in my body even as I heard it. As did Thomas Masterson: his head went up, twitching like a fox hearing a hound's cry.

Leviathan was coming.

"Now?" He turned and looked, puzzled, at the open sea around us. "But why—I haven't yet—"

"Perhaps it no longer cares what you have or have not done," I said. "Perhaps it never did."

He gave me a scathing look. "I said to put her with the other one," he snapped, seizing Madame Viart by the arm.

With a last glance at Madame Viart's stricken expression I was propelled across the deck and into a narrow hall with doors on either side. Here, my guard kept the pistol pointed at me while he fumbled for his keys. There was no one else about; everyone was crowded on deck. When he drew the ring out, he began turning it with one hand, trying to find the key he wanted.

In the distance, bells started tolling. The sound startled the man, and in that moment, I reached down, drew out Mr. Simmons' knife, and pressed it to his throat while I clamped my free hand over his mouth. "Drop the pistol," I whispered, "or I will cut your throat."

In response, he jabbed his elbow backward, but I twisted so the blow only scraped my ribs—an instinctive move, for how many times had I done so with Mr. Windham? Only, I had not held a knife then. In our grappling, his neck wrenched right and something hot and wet ran over my hand. The man struggled frenetically, trying to buck me off him as his blood spurted onto the walls and floor. I could not think but to hold on, my hand over his mouth like iron, stifling his cries. Everything was tolling bells and the muffled shouts of men and our own gasping breaths. We careened around as the boat lurched one way and we another. I felt like nothing more than a rag doll. At last, he sank to his knees, keys and pistol alike falling away. Only then did I release him.

Outside, the bells tolled unceasingly. Only a man. Only a man, in the end. Mr. Simmons' knife still gleamed with blood, and I had blood up to my elbow and spattered everywhere else. Who knew there was so much blood in a man? Only a man, perhaps one of the volunteers in those lists we had stolen, perhaps just a man wanting a day's pay.

Still the bells rang out. The alarm, I realized dully. Someone had raised the alarm in Medby. The world shimmered as I shoved the pistol in my pocket and began testing keys. I was crying; I could not stop crying. The crew were yelling at each other, men were shouting and running. My feet kept sliding in blood as one key after another refused to turn. It seemed an age since we had come back here. Why had no one else come after us? Why did no one care that he was dead?

And then the key turned and I threw the door open and flung myself against Jo, standing ready to strike me with a washing-jug.

At once she was holding me and I was holding her. She drew back and saw the blood and with a cry began feeling me everywhere until I choked out, "It's not mine," and she held me again.

"Caroline," she gasped in my ear. "Caroline, Caroline."

As if my name was a charm. There was nothing but her, nothing, and I wanted only to stay with her in that little room forever.

The cacophony of bells and men gave way to that unnatural wailing, so much closer now. We looked at the wall, as if we could see past it to the open sea.

"It's coming," I whispered, my voice shuddering.

"So soon? But we are barely away—"

"I—I thought to lure it, when we got closer to Grimsby." I forced the words out. "Only—Mister Morrow, he had the bait thrown overboard while we were weighing anchor. He knew the words—I cannot think why—"

"I think he has his own agenda," Jo said. "Can we get away?"

"No boats." My mouth was dry as I spoke. I saw the bruises mottling Jo's face, and that they had taken her coat from her. We were in some kind of empty anteroom. A chain ran from a ring in the wall to her ankle; quickly, I shook out the key ring and hunted down a plausible key.

"Did they sight it, then? Is that why they've raised the alarm?"

I tried to think. It seemed like years had passed since I was outside. "I think so. Yes."

"Then perhaps a boat will get sent out to us."

But her hopeful tone sounded forced to my ears. I smiled a little as I bent over her ankle. "Hope springs eternal?"

She laughed softly. "That we'll be spared a cold swim? Always."

I unlocked her ankle and stood again. "As long as we're together," I said.

Again, she kissed me, more slowly and sweetly. My pocket lightened and she held up the pistol. "Country girl," she whispered.

In response, I wiped the little knife on my breeches and held it ready, slipping my free hand into hers. She nudged the door open with the muzzle of the gun. The body on the floor gave her pause. She looked at me, her eyes dark with understanding, and squeezed my hand tightly before leading me past the body. I swallowed fresh tears as we made our way to the door leading to the deck.

Here again, she nudged it slightly open, only to gasp. She drew me close so I, too, could peer out.

The deck was chaos. A man was bellowing for cannons, another shouting to bring the ship about. At his command, we lurched sickeningly to the left, so deeply I feared we might capsize. When we straightened again I saw it: a massive, dark body just breaking the water before it disappeared again. Behind it, the sky was black with storm clouds. Far in the distance, lightning streaked down to touch the sea.

Two gentlemen ran past us to the other side of the boat, shouting and waving. We peeked around the doorframe, just glimpsing the coastline and Medby. Three small boats were throwing up sails and working their way out of the harbor.

"Do you think they're coming to help us?" I asked.

"Let's hope so," Jo replied. "The question is now how to get to them without getting shot, and without having to spend too long in that water—"

We were interrupted by a bellowing roar that gusted across the deck as strong as a wind, the door blowing wide open with fetid air. The Leviathan reared out of the sea in a spray of water, sending out waves that set its namesake twisting wildly. We clung to the doorframe and each other, men tumbled from the rigging into the sea, and one of the gentlemen began shooting wildly at the creature, though it was far from range. His shots struck a sailor in the shoulder and his fellows spun about, murder in their faces.

From above came the strange syllables used to control the beast, oddly amplified. We looked up to see Thomas Masterson halfway up the rigging, one arm twined in the ropes and a speaking trumpet pressed to his mouth. He shouted phrases over and over, but the beast merely dove, sending another wave cascading over the deck and drenching us all in icy water. As if an afterthought, a volley of cannon fire erupted, landing harmlessly in the sea. Somewhere, women were screaming.

"Seize them!" Masterson yelled, pointing his trumpet at the deck. "Seize the women and throw them over!"

From one of the holds, the men began drawing up the women from Madame Viart's, dragging them by limbs and hair to the side of the ship. Madame Viart came last, fighting violently. From somewhere on her person she drew out a tiny pistol and shot at Masterson, but if she struck her target, he made no sign.

"Shit," Jo hissed, peering back at Medby again. "Those boats are still too far away. If they can't swim—"

"Over there!" The crowd suddenly parted to reveal Captain Herbert grinning in triumph, his outstretched arm pointing directly at us. "Two more for the beast, lads!"

Then everything became a nightmare.

The men rushed at us, their faces contorted horribly in the deepening gloom, their fists raised. They fell upon us before we could flee, using our hiding place to their advantage.

My knife was gone in an instant. I punched and kicked and was pummeled in more ways than I thought possible. There was no time to think, no time. For every blow I blocked there were three more, for every punch I landed, I took one that shattered me. Jo was yelling curses but they were already swinging her towards the railings, and then arms seized me around the waist and tossed me high into the air like I was nothing more than a sack of flour.

There was a sickening moment when I was above it all, boat and sea alike, and I saw Thomas Masterson still shouting his words and Mr. Morrow climbing alongside him, swinging a rifle like a club to knock the trumpet away and then throwing himself on Mr. Masterson—

—then I fell headfirst into the sea.

The water was so *cold.* It torched every nerve and took my breath away. I sank into a quiet, swirling darkness streaked with dim light. I was sinking, but it did not alarm me, because I was so very sore and tired. The water pushed me one way and another like I was nothing more than a toy. My lungs ached. If I did not breathe soon, I would die, or perhaps just sleep. I was so very tired.

Below my feet, an absolute darkness welled and rose before me, a cascade of rippling tentacles atop a vast body with glistening scales. I looked into a massive yellow eye and the creature looked at me, it *saw* me. There was intelligence behind that flat surface.

Then its tentacles splayed, and the creature roared. I glimpsed a cruel mouth ringed with teeth before the force of the cry knocked me away. Though I spun through the water, the heat of its breath revived my senses. Instinctively, I flailed my arms towards the light until I broke the surface at last, gulping down air that felt like knives in my throat. Beside me, the Leviathan, the true Leviathan, rose up once more and crashed down atop its paltry namesake, snapping the ship in two. It vanished again only to surface a moment later, whipping a piece of the stern at the harbor. The whole time it was bellowing, bellowing as if in pain. When it surfaced again there were men in its tentacles that it slung into its maw and swallowed in a thrice.

In the distance, a cannon fired. I looked over my shoulder to see more ships coming from the south, dappled with flags, but as I looked the shapes began to blur. The cold was seeping through me again, bringing with it a sudden, overwhelming despair. I had no idea whether Jo lived, I had killed a man, and Madame and her women were undoubtedly dead. I was so very tired, and what would I live for? To face a life without Jo? It all seemed hopeless. Men were screaming and crying, the creature was bellowing, rain began pouring down from the lowering sky, and I was so cold and so very tired—

An arm seized me around my torso, pulling me further above the surface of the water. A large piece of wood floated before me. "Grab on, girl," Mr. Morrow said, "or we'll both be for it."

I did as I was bade, dragging myself partially atop the

wide board, so that my head and shoulders were well above the water. "You did this," I gasped, "you did this."

"Indeed I did," he said. He grasped the board on either side of me and began kicking steadily. "Sent him straight to hell as he deserved. Or were you actually planning to eat that rot?"

"We were planning to wait for the Navy," I managed to get out, kicking at the water in sudden anger.

"More of that, please." He laughed when I kicked again and gave him a look for good measure. "Well, I didn't know about your navy. I had my own plan that went rather well, I think, and I should be toasting myself now, only you sank like a stone and ended up way out here. Everyone else made the boats."

I fell silent, then: "Jo?" I scarcely dared to form her name. "Jo made it?"

"Your lady? I left her paddling towards the others. Told her she was too beaten to search for you, she'd just end up drowning."

I started crying harder.

"Kick while you're doing that, please," he grunted.

Obediently I kicked, my stiff legs warming with the movement, and slowly we crawled towards a dinghy. "What did you say to it?" I asked.

"Haven't the faintest," Mr. Morrow said. "Copied down the sounds that make it attack. Gibberish, but it always worked."

Ahead of us, a figure rose up in the bow of the dinghy, waving us closer. "But *why*?" I whispered.

"That's my damn business," Mr. Morrow growled.

"Captain Herbert—he said you were a slave—"

"Hunt was an asshole," Mr. Morrow said, "and my father's a grocer in Cheapside."

And then I was looking up into the tired, relieved face of Mr. Windham, holding out hands to both of us, and I gave myself over to my exhaustion.

CHAPTER XVI

Endings, and Beginnings

Of the ensuing chaos, I later remembered little, so dazed was I with cold and exhaustion. The Navy ships—for it was the Navy I had glimpsed to the south, bearing down upon us—opened fire on the beast, but it simply dove again and did not reappear. Only later would I learn that it had kept to Thomas Masterson's plan, reappearing where the Thames opened into the Channel, where our navy was having a tense standoff with the French force that had moved north from Calais. Its appearance made enemies into temporary allies, and between them they managed to drive it off with only a few ships damaged, and a handful of casualties.

Then it vanished.

I was rowed to the nearest of the Medby boats, with Mr. Windham pouring explanations into my ear: they had found the body of the real Captain Herbert, whereupon he had ridden for Medby while Mr. Smith and the Navy ships made ready to intercept the *Leviathan*. On the road, he had crossed paths with Mr. Simmons and sent him on while he pressed on to aid us—only to find my father and Mrs. Lambert rallying the remaining sailors of Medby.

For it was my father, my dear, brave father, who had been

standing on the roof of Mrs. Lambert's sister's alehouse, despite the biting cold, watching the *Leviathan* through our old spyglass—and saw the barrels being emptied out the back of the ship, and knew something had gone wrong. How he had convinced Mrs. Lambert, and by extension the men of Medby, to raise the alarm against Thomas Masterson, I would never know. By the time Mr. Windham arrived, the first bells were already tolling and all Mr. Windham had to do was help organize the men into a productive rescue.

At the time, much of this speech was lost on me, for as sensation returned, I found I could not breathe without pain. Before I knew what was happening, I was hustled into the ship's hold and swathed in a large number of coats and blankets, then laid atop a reeking table while a man claiming to be a doctor took my pulse and Mr. Windham chafed my hands and feet. A bottle was pressed to my lips while hands felt my body. Something was said about my ribs as I swallowed what turned out to be a most foul rum.

"Miss Daniels," Mr. Windham was saying, "this fellow Morrow, what of him?"

I blinked, trying to focus on Mr. Windham as the doctor cut away my clothes. "He killed Thomas Masterson," I said, "and he saved us."

It seemed, in the moment, a profound assessment of all that had happened.

After that, everything took on the hazy quality of a dream. My next waking thought was that I was swathed in bandages, wearing the clothes of a man who was unfamiliar with bathing, and somehow wedged into a hammock from which

I could in no way extricate myself. This seemed a perfect time to go back to sleep, and I did.

When I next woke up, it was to Jo's worried face hovering over me. With a cry, I worked free an arm and pulled her to me. All was breathless kissing, the warmth of her, the smell—

"I was so afraid," Jo said into my neck. "I couldn't see you anywhere and then that bloody Morrow said he would fetch you, and I couldn't think—"

"I thought you were dead," I blurted out, only to be smothered in kisses again. When at last we broke apart, I whispered, "I want to go home."

The warm smile she gave me made my throat close. "And we shall, my darling. We're in Medby harbor, we were just waiting for you to wake up of your own accord. Mister Smith has paid out handsomely, and Mister Simmons has started on arrangements while Missus Simmons looks after your father—"

"Missus Simmons?" I was crying again, when had I not been crying? I felt as if I could just weep, weep for the rest of my days.

"It seems she arrived yesterday and in the midst of the alarm managed to find your father—I'll never speak ill of her nosiness again." At my weak smile, Jo's expression warmed. "She managed to calm him when the *Leviathan* sank and helped Doctor Denham create a hospital right there in the alehouse. She even hugged me when I was brought ashore …"

At that I could take no more. I flung my arms around Jo and sobbed while she hushed me and held me close. The doctor murmured something and Jo nodded, but I clung to her harder and she did not let go. "He thinks you're hysterical," she whispered. "But the fool wasn't there. You just cry, darling. Cry for both of us."

In the end, we could not go home, at least not right away, for it snowed heavily while I was recovering and the roads became impassable. Thus, the Simmonses took a room with Mrs. Lambert and Mrs. Simmons set about making a decent Christmas for us in the tiny cottage. I spent much of my day in bed, dozing to the sound of my father's pen as he wrote Jo and I little stories about my childhood. Often, he would look to me, as if wanting me to speak, but I could not. To tell him that what haunted my dreams was not the monster nor the ship breaking apart, but the feel of a man dying by my hand—I could not speak of it, not to him.

I did speak to Jo, but her staunch defense of my actions did nothing to ease the sickening memory. It was an accident, save that I had a knife pressed to the man's throat. He would have done the same to me, save that he had not. *Anyone bringing a weapon to a confrontation expects to use it*, Mr. Windham had told me all those weeks ago, and hadn't I thrown myself at Harold Owston like an animal? At times I found myself staring at my hands as if they belonged to some other creature, a far fouler being than the Caroline Daniels I had thought myself.

Seeing that her arguments were having little effect, Jo set herself to distracting me instead with news of the various players in our adventure. The *Leviathan* was being written off as all hands lost, though someone had returned to Mr. Masterson's building and taken the ledgers—and the painting as well. Madame Viart and her women had vanished the moment they reached shore. The brothel remained locked and silent, and all of Medby seemed united in pretending it had never existed. Of Mr. Morrow, we knew only that he had been taken by the Navy for questioning. Mr. Smith wrote us letters, telling us of the monster's actions in the Channel and the subsequent inquiries into Thomas Masterson's many accomplices, but he never addressed our pleas on Mr. Morrow's behalf. We feared he might face transportation or worse.

I attended church on Christmas Eve, only to be so overwhelmed by guilt that I wept through the night on Jo's shoulder. She made my excuses for Christmas Day service, and after repeated assurances that I just needed rest, went with the others. Thus, for the first time since it all happened I was alone, but the solitude only seemed to cast my memories into sharper relief. I felt again and again the blood on my hands, and the sense of life fleeing from a body, until I thought I was going mad. When a knock came, I flew to open the door, half-expecting an angel of judgment come down upon me at last—

—only to find myself gaping at Mr. Morrow, who raised his eyebrows at my panicked expression.

"I was passing," he said, "and thought to see if you survived."

I stared at him, shocked and teary-eyed. With a sigh, he

stepped inside, pushing me into the front room and shutting the door behind us. "What's wrong?" he asked. "And where's the other one?"

I should have gathered my wits and calmed myself, but instead I found myself pouring out the story to him. "Only, I cannot sleep now," I gasped. "Every time I close my eyes, it is there, every time I see a, a piece of *meat* I think of the blood. In church, I feel everyone *knows*—"

"Stop it," Mr. Morrow cut in, visibly irritated. "Good God, woman. Men die all the time, far more painfully and for far worse reasons. Cutler made a choice to side with Masterson, and he made the wrong choice. That's all there is to it."

"But I *killed* him," I said, enunciating the word, did he not understand? "I killed him in cold blood. There is no exculpating such a crime. I may be *damned*."

Again, Mr. Morrow only sighed. "If I told you of Cutler's reprehensible character, would that make it easier to bear? What if he had orders to shoot you both, then and there, and toss your bodies overboard? Would knowing that help?" Before I could speak, he raised a finger at me. "Words like *damn* and *sin* are men's words. Your soul is God's business. I'm not going to presume to think for Him and neither should you. Leave men's words to men and your soul to God."

I frowned at him. "Is that what you do?"

"It has not failed me yet."

"Even though you brought the monster down upon your own crew?"

Mr. Morrow leaned against a chair, smiling now. "Even though." When I only shook my head, he sighed yet again, but it was a gentler sound. "I will tell you this much, Missus: in Thomas Masterson's eyes, we were all nothing more than *inventory*, just tally marks in a book. He sank a full slaver to regain control of the Leviathan, and that was nowhere near the worst of his dealings. As for the rest, that's between God and myself. He knows my reasons and He's the only one who gets to judge me for them."

The church bells began pealing then, startling us both. Mr. Morrow laughed. "A sign from above?" He touched his hat. "You'll be fine," he added, going to the door.

I followed, trying to find words for my confused thoughts, but he opened the door to reveal everyone returning for dinner: my father between Mrs. Simmons and Mrs. Lambert, laughing aloud; Mr. Simmons in conversation with Mr. Windham; and behind them all, Jo walking arm-in-arm with a slight, dark figure in a rich blue greatcoat that made him stand out against the grey stone.

Mr. Smith raised his hat as Jo said delightedly, "So, no prison for you, Morrow?" and Mrs. Simmons cried, "*Another* guest? Think of the goose!"

"No goose for me," Mr. Morrow said as he greeted the party. "I sail at first light."

Mr. Smith helped my father inside, touching my hand in greeting and smiling warmly as he did so, though he was hurried along by Mrs. Simmons, who desired to assess our vegetables with Mrs. Lambert's help.

"I take it you're bound for other lands?" Jo asked, a gleam in her eye.

"A mutual friend has made me an offer." He smiled then,

a warm smile, not the cold expression he had worn in Mr. Masterson's employ. "It seems she may have work for me, and I've never been to France."

"Take care," Mr. Windham said in a low voice. "We've seen how playing sides can end."

Mr. Morrow looked significantly past us. I glanced over my shoulder to see Mr. Smith at the end of the hall. He nodded once and Mr. Morrow did the same. "Never fear, sir," he said to Mr. Windham. "I know on which side my bread is buttered." And with that, he took his leave, though not without a last admonishing look in my direction.

And then all was the flurry of Christmas, and I had no time to think on it further. There was the goose to see to, and the vegetables, and much running to and fro. Mrs. Simmons and Jo got into an argument about the seating, for Jo was set on us breaking bread together while Mrs. Simmons demanded a return to propriety. Yet, just as I feared a recurrence of their antagonism, Mrs. Simmons simply said, "Well, it is Christmas I suppose," and put Mr. Smith and Mr. Windham to setting the table.

Mrs. Lambert went to her sister's but promised to be back for pudding. Dr. Denham sent word he would stop by with a bottle of port for my father. Mr. Windham kept us laughing all through the cooking with stories about his youth with Mr. Smith, for they had begun their army careers together.

Thus, when I finished dressing for dinner and found the table laden, my father already beaming at one end and Jo seated in her best suit at the other, the deep grief inside me eased. My soul was God's business and no other, and wasn't that the right of it? I was ushered into my seat at Jo's right by Mr. Simmons, who then set to carving. When I looked at Mrs. Simmons sitting across from me, her eyes were glistening. We had not truly spoken since she returned, but her expression gave me hope that we might do so.

Mr. Smith poured the wine. Mr. Simmons carved the goose. Jo took my hand and kissed it, and no one flinched. I thought then that it might just be possible to be truly happy in this life.

It was late, very late, after dinner and pudding, charades and songs, that Jo and I wearily climbed into bed. As we drew the covers over our heads, Jo whispered, "Think of the goose!" and I burst out laughing, really laughing, as I had not done in days. For it had all somehow come out right, born of pain and grief, but somehow richer for it, every touch of skin to skin the foundation of our future, every press of her lips to mine a happiness I could only pray to be worthy of. Would that all the world could be as we were.

Misses Chase and Daniels return in

The Painter's Widow

ACKNOWLEDGEMENTS

Readers familiar with the Yorkshire coast might recognize aspects of the fictional town of Medby, which is based on Scarborough. A family event last fall offered the rare opportunity to see the coastline I had envisioned for *Leviathan*, and Scarborough's unique landscape proved irresistible. I am indebted to the Scarborough Archaeological and Historical Society, and especially Keith Johnston, for accommodating our last-minute visit. Keith's expert tour helped me to see the Georgian Scarborough hidden behind the Victorian promenade; the wealth of scholarly material the Society provided grounded the story in lore and detail. I am deeply grateful for their invaluable aid.

As always, this book would not have been possible without the labor of so many others. Kat Howard provided expert editorial guidance and helped me see the forest for the trees. Liz Bourke gave the kind of close, sensitive reading that is a boon to all writers. Charlotte Ashley did what she could to tame my grammar; any errors in this book are solely my stubbornness. Najla and Nada Qamber created the cover and interior respectively. Lastly, my spouse provided time, solitude, and patience, endured my doubts and frustrations, and always kept the porch light on.

ABOUT THE AUTHOR

L.S. Johnson was born in New York and now lives in California, where she feeds her cats by writing book indexes. Her stories have appeared in such venues as *Strange Horizons*, *Interzone*, *Long Hidden: Speculative Fiction from the Margins of History*, and *Year's Best Weird Fiction*. Her collection, *Vacui Magia: Stories*, won the 2nd Annual North Street Book Prize and was a finalist for the World Fantasy Award. To learn about new stories and upcoming appearances, and for exclusive excerpts, updates, and more, sign up for her newsletter at www.traversingz.com.